Iter
on or

GLOU
LI
TE'

LOVER'S LEAP

Based on the Jamaican Legend

Horane Smith

MINERVA PRESS

ATLANTA LONDON SYDNEY

LOVER'S LEAP: *Based on the Jamaican Legend*
Copyright © Horane Smith 1999

All Rights Reserved

ISBN 0 75410 589 X

First Published 1999 by
MINERVA PRESS
315–317 Regent Street
London W1R 7YB

Printed in Great Britain for Minerva Press

LOVER'S LEAP
Based on the Jamaican Legend

This is a work of fiction and while it is based on a popular legend, some characters have been introduced into the story to make it more credible.

To my wife Beverley,
Sheyhu, Samar, Jordi, Codi, my entire family
and all those people who encouraged me

Chapter One

The burnt-out cane field sprawled mercilessly under the summer sun. It was another hot, miserable, and long Monday afternoon for Jerome Scott. The day was the 23rd August 1830; a day Jerome wished would end as quickly as he had seen the penetrating rays of the sun peep through his half-broken window early in the morning and then disappear.

Sweat trickled down his forehead. The salty liquid wormed its way alongside his left ear, and crept into the corner of his sealed lips. The lips parted as they lusted after anything in liquid form. They were parched, cracked, and dry from lack of water.

Jerome was a slave. He couldn't drink as he would have liked, despite the abundance of water on the Caribbean island. He was the youngest – twenty-two years old of thirty males and ten females, who worked the sugar plantation of Alfred Campbell, a rich English land baron. 'Jack's Place', named after his brother, who had died six months ago, consisted of one hundred and ten acres of arable land, and was situated on the southern most tip of Jamaica's south coast in what is now known as the parish of St Elizabeth. The district was called 'Big Yard', while for others, it was known as 'Yardley Chase'.

Big Yard was an appropriate name. There were about three huge houses on plantations in the district, all with big outdoors, which served several different purposes, from dishing out meals to whipping. Yardley Chase was ideal too. Plantation owners faced challenging times coping with runaway slaves; whenever a slave was discovered escaping sometimes it resulted in a chase. Older slaves and the ones who were more conscious about the growing resentment to slavery, preferred the latter.

'The sun is going down,' snapped the burly figure of the plantation's foreman, John Stewart. 'C'mon you lazy bums, it will be four long hours before sunset,' his voice squeaking in order to be loud enough to be heard by the long line of slaves at the other end of the field. 'You want supper… food tonight?' he queried.

There was no answer. Slaves knew it was a cardinal sin to answer without being asked to.

The angry crack of the thin, snake-like whip echoed in Jerome's ear. A red-faced John lashed it several times in anticipation of faster movement from the machetes, as they swung from above heads into the slender cane plants leaning against one another.

Jerome had heard that sound ever so often. His greasy, sweaty hands tightened around the machete. He chopped like he was on the last row of plants; a thousand plants must have felt that blade since daybreak.

'Move faster you wretches… remember, no work, no supper!' he yelled, his voice informing everyone that he was in command.

Anger tingled throughout Jerome's body to such an extent that he felt he had the guts to go over to where John was and turn his fat face the other way around. But he could hear a voice saying, 'Wait! The time is not yet.' He had heard that voice on more than one occasion. Could it be that of his father he wondered.

Jerome only knew his father as Kofi. He knew very little about him, except to say that his ancestors came from the Ashanti tribe from along Africa's west coast. The last time he saw him, Jerome was ten years old. Kofi was sold when the plantation that owned him changed hands. He remembered the agony of being separated from his father and forced to remain with his mother, who had been very sickly. She passed away two years later.

It had been a lonely life for Jerome; a woman, no relative of his, took care of him until he was about eighteen and able to survive the misery of plantation life. He had heard on the grapevine that his father was working on a plantation at the other end of the island – about one hundred and twenty miles away. Jerome grew with hate in his heart. He had no friends, except Maude Barrow, his foster mother. Jerome hated the world.

'Move! move! You lazy bums,' the froth-mouthed John continued. 'You!' he said, pointing at Jerome. 'Get over here at once!'

Jerome wasn't certain if John meant him. He pointed questioningly at himself.

'You of course,' John grinned, his tobacco-stained teeth becoming visible through parted lips. 'You lazy wretch.'

Lazy was John's password, but to say that Jerome was that kind of character was sheer dishonesty. Jerome knew there was trouble. The two hundred-pound foreman had been chewing fire all morning, seizing on every opportunity to spew his venom and foul breath in the eighty-degree heat. Jerome had only paused for a few seconds to watch the cane plant, an unusually big one, fall helplessly to the ground. John's cold, piercing eyes darted to where he was standing. They had hit their target, an undeserving target.

The young slave stepped forward nervously, his knees wobbling under his dirt-soaked trousers. Jerome was about five feet, eleven inches tall, weighed about one hundred and twenty pounds, and was athletic in outlook. He had a small, pleasant face – his dark features more pronounced on his hands and face because of sunburn. He was ruggedly handsome and with adequate care, could get the attention of any young woman. There was something about his calm composure which made him noticeable. Then again, that could be detrimental to him, given the style of life on the plantation.

'For refusing to work, you will sleep at Hell House tonight,' John told Jerome, when he was about six feet from him.

Jerome stopped in his tracks.

'Get back to work or else I will make that two nights,' John grinned.

Hell House was an area a lot of slaves feared, especially the older ones. It was a huge star apple tree with some chains around it. For punishment, a slave was chained to it and had to sleep there through the night, whether there was rain or storm. During the star apple season, which had just ended, it was not used for that purpose for fear that slaves would feast on the fruits. The common enemy this time of the year was not rain or storm, it was mosquitoes, and sometimes sandflies.

Jerome felt like a mule had kicked him in the face. A mere pause had caused him a night at Hell House. Nevertheless, it would be his second time there, and like the first he would try to make the best of it by gazing at the bright stars in the heavens until he fell sleep.

Reluctantly, he returned to his work. The sun felt hotter now; his stomach churned and it reminded him that he could not afford to lose supper, so he had to put out his best.

The huge orange ball of fire edged towards the horizon. The weary souls chopped away, each ear waiting to hear the voice of John Stewart saying another day had ended. It didn't take long for him to give the command, and when he did the sun was no longer visible.

Supper was a bowl of cornmeal porridge and a slice of home-made bread. He could hardly wait to place his hand on the old, rusty bowl after standing in the line-up for so long. Within five minutes the food disappeared. As soon as he had had a cup of water, a grinning John grabbed him by the shoulder and steered him towards Hell House.

The other slaves, notably his elderly talking partner, Babwe, watched them move towards the star apple tree. Babwe looked into the sky. It would be a beautiful night. He smiled.

*

Anita Campbell was bored to death. Since she joined her father on the island, about a year ago, her new life had been a challenge. She rarely saw anyone in her age group; where were they?

Anita's mother, Lynda, should have been there by now. But the ships leaving London, England, had been too crowded over the past six months. Bad weather in the Atlantic as well as increased traffic between Jamaica and England had been major factors in the overcrowding. Sugar was king; Jamaica happened to be one of England's biggest producers. Lynda was planning to leave before the winter.

Life in the tropics had not been what the twenty-two year old Anita had expected. There were many surprises. She never imagined that her father, the kind, gentle and humble man, who left England two years ago for the West Indies, had become so heartless and greedy – to have those poor blacks working in the sun all day long, with little food. She felt sick when the thought of their ordeal came to mind.

On the other hand, Alfred was a good father. He had been encouraging her to return to England to study and then come back to take up a position at one of those all-white schools in Spanish Town or nearby Kingston. Anita had been giving it serious thought until John, the foreman, walked right into her life and snatched all her plans away, at least for a while. He had provided comfort during lonely times and had been a good talking companion. She wished though that he was a little younger, he being thirty, and not so fat. In this sun-drenched land, where the slave population vastly outnumbered whites, Anita had little choice.

Undoubtedly, Anita was a beautiful woman; she could get any young man she wanted. Medium-built, nicely tanned, evenly curved lips and sparkling brown eyes, Anita had it all. She suspected her father knew of the relationship, but whether or not he did, sooner or later it would come out in public. John wanted an early marriage. Anita often thought about that too, and had concluded that marriage and children could be just what she wanted.

John would not be sneaking by tonight to supposedly visit her father to discuss what had transpired in the field. It was Monday and Alfred always had meetings with nearby plantation owners. From what she could glean from the closed-door talks, a slavery rebellion was not too far-fetched. A number of plantation owners had been living with that nightmare. She didn't give it much thought, except to say that she had a good relationship with all the slave women who looked after the house.

Anita stepped out into the cool of the night. A huge full moon crawled up from behind the hills, spreading silver beams across the quiet yard. The stars were out already; they twinkled in the brightly-lit sky, illuminating the entire surroundings as if it was the break of day.

She walked towards the well where she normally sat on some of her nightly strolls. She sat quietly, her white dress glistening in the moonlight. Hell House was only a few yards from the well. The sound of a chain startled her just as she was about to enter her world of thoughts and dreams.

Anita spun around to face the tree. The shadow formed

under the tree made it a little difficult to see if there was anything there. The sound came again. This time Anita stepped backward. Her heart raced faster, she waited for a few seconds, her eyes starting to recognise the figure of a person, sitting up with his back against the tree.

'I-is someone there?' she asked nervously. There was no answer. 'A-answer me… is someone there?' she said, moving one step closer.

'Y-yes 'um,' came a hesitant reply.

'What are you doing there?' said Anita, still somewhat nervous. 'Are you all right?'

'I-I am sleepin' here.'

'What? Why?' She moved closer, to where she could almost see him clearly. 'Why are you sleeping here?' Anita had always seen the chains under the tree, but not for one moment had she ever thought they were used to shackle slaves, and worst of all, while they slept outdoors.

'Mr John is punishin' me ma'am.'

'Punishing you? What for?'

'He said I was lazy ma'am.'

'Are you?'

'No ma'am. I work very hard.'

'I believe you all work hard,' said she, earnestly. 'Isn't it cold out here?' She could see the tiredness in his face, yet there was a certain warmth and sincerity about it.

Oh, those poor people, she thought. What a life. She could see those eyes glistening in the glow of the full moon. He seemed relaxed and willing to obey his master. The innocent-looking face that peered at her made Anita shiver from something she wasn't certain about. Guilt? Maybe, or could it be an inner concern she always had for the poor and oppressed. She didn't know that concern was there until she saw the wretched life of these slaves. Each day her sorrows multiplied, especially whenever she confronted an unfortunate situation. Somehow, this one seemed exceptional.

Anita had observed men being tied to a tree and whipped, teenage girls secretly and reluctantly fulfilling the sexual desires of white men, women and men being sold like merchandise, not to mention the horrible state of their living quarters. How could her father sleep with a clear conscience? Lynda had only heard of the horror stories, Anita wondered what her reaction would be when she saw it with her very own eyes.

She turned towards the house and glancing up into the heavens she whispered, 'Dear God, deliver these people.' A tear crawled down her cheek when she turned the door knob to the living room. She stopped in the doorway and looked towards the star apple tree. Underneath the tree was darkened by the shadows, preventing her from seeing anything. A small gust of wind coming from 'Lookout' stirred the front section of her hair.

Lookout was a popular spot, not only for her, but for the entire community. Big Yard was about one thousand feet above sea level, the highest and most scenic spot being Lookout. Lookout provided a breathtaking and panoramic view of the south coast stretching for about fifty miles from east to west. Looking southward, ships could be spotted about forty miles out in the Caribbean Sea. But the real beauty came when you looked from the peak down to the shoreline about three miles below, as the mountain range gradually descended down into the sea. Lookout was the ultimate for relaxation, sightseeing and meditation. Of late, it had become a popular place for young lovers, even Anita herself.

Tonight could get cold, Anita thought. She marched to her room and grabbed a blanket from the closet and returned to the star apple tree with it. She gave no thought to her action.

Jerome was still sitting up. He watched her approach.

She saw the stern but calm look on his face as she drew nearer. It was as if he wanted to say something but didn't have the guts to do it.

'Here, take this,' she said, reaching out with the blanket.

Jerome stared at her, not knowing what to do.

'Here, take it… you'll need it.'

Again, Jerome made no move. He feared something and she knew it now.

'I know you could get into trouble… but…'

'I can't ma'am.'

'Please…'

'No ma'am. I-it's not so cold tonight ma'am.'

'I will tell Dad you were sick,' she said, putting down the blanket beside him.

'I can't take it ma'am.'

'But I want you to have it.' A broad smile rippled across her face. 'Here is a deal. What time do you get up in the morning?'

'Five thirty.'

'Okay, I will be back before five thirty and no one will know you have it. But how do you know when it's five thirty?'

Jerome smiled for the first time. It came across to her like a fulfilled wish.

'When the rooster crows the second time around.'

Anita laughed, almost aloud. She had heard the roosters in the morning but never knew they were used to designate time by the slaves. 'I hope they wake me tomorrow morning,' she said, teasingly.

'But s-s-suppose you don't come and get it?'

'Just fold it up and throw it behind the well,' she grinned.

He smiled again. This time around it must have been the warmest smile she had seen in a long time. She found it strange though; why should a slave be having such an impact on her? Her father would be outraged if he knew what was happening there now. She must be going mad. Did she realise what she was doing? Anita, come to your senses! Those questions echoed in her head. When she couldn't face the situation any more, she told him good night, and walked away towards the house, almost in a run.

Although the questions rang in her head, she had an uncontrollable feeling that somehow, somewhere, she wanted to see Jerome again.

Chapter Two

It was past midnight. Jerome had fallen asleep sitting up; the last thing he remembered was watching the moon disappearing in the thick foliage of leaves. Under the tree it had become darker then, so it must have been somewhere around that time that he dozed off.

So far, the night had not been that bad. For one, no mosquitoes greeted him and most importantly, he had been given a wonderful piece of comfort by an unexpected visitor, whatever her name was.

Jerome's thoughts raced towards her now. His eyes moved from underneath the tree to the huge, white and imposing mansion of Jack's Place. That was where his unusual and friendly visitor came from about four hours ago. Was he dreaming? The warm blanket reminded him otherwise.

Her name – Jerome tried to recall what it was but to no avail. On more than one occasion he had heard talk among the womenfolk of their new mistress. From what he could remember, she was always discussed in good light; she was kind-hearted and saw no reason why the slaves should be treated in such a degrading manner.

He remembered her pale skin looking ghost-like in the moonlight. Her friendliness was beyond belief. He, a poor, underprivileged slave, had the attention of the daughter of his owner, for at least fifteen minutes. Furthermore, he was certain that the blanket he had been given belonged to her. She must have used it at least once. What did all that mean?

It was on that thought that tiredness got hold of him and he fell asleep again.

Anita didn't go to bed until after midnight. She was up and about the house finding all kinds of things to occupy her mind. She was concerned that she could get Jerome into serious trouble, which even she might be unable to shield him from. However, she was confident her plan would work.

The meeting between her father and other owners was not over yet. The light in the living room was on and she could hear voices. It was only then she realised what a chance she had taken when she brought the blanket to Jerome. She could have been seen. But, judging from the shouts and howls of disagreement, the meeting seemed rather too interesting for anyone to have left.

Anita was fixing a cup of tea when she heard the door open and footsteps trekking away towards the front door. She didn't move from her position until all the voices had faded from inside to outside. Before she could leave the kitchen Alfred walked in.

'Hey, what are you doing up so late?' he said, a bit startled at her presence.

'I went for a walk earlier and I was about to go to bed.'

'Oh. It's really a nice night – maybe I should go for a walk too.'

'No Dad, it's too late for that now. You must be tired,' she said nervously.

'In fact, I am not. Look at the moon, it is so beautiful... the stars... what beauty,' he said, after walking over to the window and parting the curtain.

The star apple tree was clearly visible from that vantage point. That beige-coloured blanket could be seen on this silvery night. She stepped over towards her father, wanting to distract him from looking any further.

'Dad, will the slaves rebel?' she asked.

Alfred's hand dropped from the curtain in amazement. Where did that question come from? Surely not from Anita whom he wanted to be the last person to ever entertain such a thought. He walked over to her, his face as serious as a judge.

Anita watched him stroll towards her. Somehow, the question must have made him look older tonight. The wrinkles around his mouth could be seen more clearly in the dim light of the kitchen. Nearing fifty, Alfred had aged in the last few years. His hair, beard and moustache all had tinges of grey; wrinkles were forming around his eyes. Alfred was a tall man, well built, and would have been a credit to heavyweight boxing, had he entered that field and was as skilful as he looked. Years of sunburn gave him bronzed features, his eyes as piercing as a king cobra. Anita bore a slight resemblance to her father. It was evident whenever they were beside each other.

'Oh honey, whatever gave you those thoughts?' he said, coming close enough to stroke her hair. 'Slaves rebelling; where did you get that idea from?'

'A... I have been wondering about these late night meetings over the past few months.'

'Meetings? But there's so much to discuss. We haven't been discussing slave rebellion any more than we have bean trying to get a better price for our sugar.'

'Don't you think the slaves are becoming more conscious?'

'How? Why should they?'

'I have heard about a movement in the east where they have been meeting secretly,' she said, watching the look on his face.

If Alfred had been sitting he would probably have jumped to his feet. Anita saw his face redden, either with fright or with anger.

'Where did you hear that Anita? Why are you bothering

yourself with something which may never happen?'

She had heard it through whisperings among the slaves, but she dared not say it. 'I heard it in Malvern.'

Malvern was the nearest big town. She had been there a few times to shop for clothes and scarce food items. The smaller towns nearby didn't sell the type of clothes she wanted, hence her father didn't hesitate to send her there.

'Maybe you should stop going there.'

'Stop. C'mon Dad. There's no harm in hearing.'

'But you are confusing yourself unnecessarily with all this dreaming about slave rebellion.'

'Okay Dad, maybe I overreacted. Let's forget the question.'

'You have me worried now.'

'C'mon. You don't have to—'

'You know what Anita, please watch how you deal with those slave girls. You don't know what may happen. As for the men, please stay far from them.'

'I thought you said there was nothing to worry about.'

'I am just being cautious, honey. I don't want you to feel threatened.'

'I will be fine.'

'If ever there was a rebellion – I must emphasise that there won't be any – but if ever there should be one, the first people slave men would be coming for is our women: wives, mothers, sisters and daughters; they could harm you all. Just bear that in mind.'

Anita knew then he was worried and had been avoiding her knowing what was going on. She thought of Jerome and the look on his face. Was she being deceived?

★

Jerome slept like a newborn baby. He couldn't recall ever sleeping like that. Never! He cuddled under the blanket all through the night; a part of it was used as a substitute for a mattress. The first time the cock crowed he didn't hear it; the second time he did. Not knowing it was the second or the first, and with no sign of Anita, he quickly slipped out of the blanket.

The heavy chains put some pressure on his wrists each time he tried to roll the blanket. But in the end it took him less than two minutes. He stood up, trying to make as little noise as possible, and got a good grip on the blanket. It was a good thing the well was not that far away, and that the back part of it, where no one ever visited, was facing him. Probably the chains would make some noise now –however, he couldn't avoid that, Jerome made one step backwards and hurled the blanket as hard as he could. It pierced the cool morning air, gliding weightlessly into the brick wall of the well and then falling behind a small clump of bushes beside it. Perfect. Nevertheless, it took him another minute to realise that the situation would only be perfect for as long as it was not discovered by someone else. The morning was dark; the moon had disappeared behind the hills to the west, but for searching eyes it wouldn't be that difficult to spot something like that behind the well. He hoped the kind young lady would keep her promise and come early to retrieve it.

Jerome looked across the slave lodgings hidden behind the trees not too far way. He could see lights twinkling in the dimly-lit windows. People were up already, getting prepared for another rigorous day. As soon as the sun edged over the hills John and the other hands would sound the alarm. They would all get a quick bowl of porridge and then head to those damp cane fields – damp from the heavy dew which fell at this time of the year. The morning portion of the day was the best. The cool air was a blessing in disguise. Many of the slaves would hum a song as they worked. As soon as the sun started to blaze down on them that was a different matter altogether. It was then that misery began.

It wouldn't make sense for Jerome to go back to sleep. Very soon, John or Peter Walter, a supervisor, would come over to unshackle him. He leaned against the tree again and started to think about the most unusual visit he had had earlier in the night.

★

Once again, it was another miserable day for Jerome. Most of the time he kept looking over his shoulders to see if someone was coming to get him. He feared that someone might find the blanket and accuse him of stealing it. Or could the young miss have framed him? The thoughts ran through his head. He was troubled. At the end of the day, Babwe saw the puzzle on his face.

'What is it that is troubling you my son?' he asked, almost in a whisper.

'Huh? Nothing is wrong,' said Jerome, not looking in his direction.

'I know you too long to ever believe that.'

'This time you are wrong.'

'I won't stop pestering you until I get the truth,' he said. His stare was fixed on him.

Jerome saw it and knew he meant what he said. 'Okay, last night was the best sleep I ever had, probably in my lifetime.'

'How? Best sleep… so why should you worry then?'

'I am worried about what caused the sleep.'

'What was that?'

'A nice, warm blanket.'

'Blanket? I have never slept in a blanket. Where in the world did you ever get that?'

'Massa's daughter.'

'What?' He stopped in his tracks but quickly started walking again when Jerome didn't stop. 'Are you begging for trouble? Did you ask her for a blanket? You must be crazy young man. Look at me! Are you crazy?' His voice sounded a little louder because of concern.

Jerome waited until he had finished his mouthful and decided to calm Babwe's fears. 'She gave it to me,' he said simply.

'She gave it to you? How?'

'She was going for a walk and saw me under the tree.'

'Just like that?'

'C'mon Babwe, which other way she could have seen me? She felt the night would be cold, disappeared and then came back with a blanket. Could I refuse it?'

'If it is going to cause you trouble, yes.'

'But what trouble?'

'You tell me, that is what you are worried about, isn't it?'

'I had to hide it behind the well. That is what I am worried about… if someone found it. She had promised to come back and get it early morning but she never did.'

Babwe grinned sheepishly. 'I tell you what. If someone had found it, you would be in deep trouble now.'

'Suppose it is still there now?'

'It is not. I said there would be big trouble.'

'Why did she give me that blanket?'

'Hmmnn. She likes you,' he teased. Jerome didn't answer because he saw that as a remote possibility. In fact, that would be bigger trouble. He had heard stories of slaves being killed for laying eyes on white women. If they had been killed for just that, then he could imagine what it would be for something deeper.

★

Anita had been marching around the living room all

afternoon, waiting for her father to bolt through the front door in his usual powerful manner. After a hard day's work there was nothing to him like coming home for a nice, cold and long bath, and then having a chat with his daughter whenever he had the time. Lynda's absence was noticeable in the evening routine and Anita watched as he counted down the days.

Anita had something up her sleeve. For the entire day she worked out a plan; a plan that could change her entire lifestyle, and ultimately, could affect or have an impact on some people, including her parents.

She got up a little earlier than usual this morning but somehow didn't have the strength to go for the blanket Jerome used. A suspicious-looking Maude handed it to her later in the day without asking what it had been doing there. Anita barely mumbled that she had been sitting on it down by the well and had forgotten to take it up. Maude looked at her from the corner of her eyes; she knew Anita was lying.

But that didn't bother Anita. What bothered her was how her father would react to what she would be requesting from him. There was a knock on the door. Anita's heart slipped a beat, a little nervousness coming over her. She turned the door knob. It couldn't be Dad; he would have a key. The burly figure of John blocked the doorway, a broad grin on his face.

'Hi honey,' he said, grinning even more.

'Hi John. I was not expecting you.' She stepped out of the way, allowing him to come inside. Disappointment was in her voice but John was too happy to see her to ever detect the difference.

'I thought I'd just come by to keep you company. Do you mind?'

'No, not at all.'

'Is your father home yet?'

'No. I am expecting him any time now.'

'So how have you been keeping? I have been so busy with those lazy bums that I am too tired even to eat.'

Anita felt anger permeating her veins when John mentioned lazy bums. She tried to control her anger. 'Don't you think you have been a little too hard on them John?'

He spun around. Was he hearing right? 'W-what... what are you saying Anita? They are slaves – that is their worth and nothing else. They are here to serve their masters.'

'But—'

'With all due respect Anita, have you been hearing those stories too, or have you been talking with some of the rebellious ones?'

Anita's face turned pink.

John wished he could have withdrawn that statement, but it was too late. 'Look. I am sorry, I should not have asked you that.'

'It's okay John,' she said quietly. 'For your information I have heard nothing of the sort. Let's forget we ever had this argument.'

'That's fine with me. By the way, about that dance Saturday night, would you like to go with me?'

Anita saw the invitation coming but part of her plan would take care of that. 'Sure. I would be happy to.'

'We will have a nice time, honey,' he said smiling. 'I promise you that. Anyway I got to go. I will be by before Saturday.' He gave her a kiss on the cheek and walked out of the room.

Anita smiled as she heard herself saying happy riddance. Why did she say that? she wondered.

Chapter Three

Maude thought like a judge. She examined her case from all sides before making any judgement. But she had a problem. The pieces of the puzzle wouldn't fit. Hence, something was missing.

That mysterious blanket had been haunting her all day. Why should it anyway? She wished she knew; and the more she thought about it, the more she became confused.

She had no doubts that Anita's story was far from the truth. But why would she lie to her? Maude was her slave, and despite their mother–daughter relationship, it was really none of her business. On the contrary, it was a challenge not to find out what the blanket was doing at the well. Jerome had only slept a few yards away from it. What made Maude even more interested was the way in which the blanket was found. It wasn't folded neatly like someone had been sitting on it. Any ten year old could have drawn the conclusion that it was thrown there. It was lying on top of some arrowroot plants like a strong wind had blown it there. The clothes line was at the other end of the yard, so it could not have been blown all the way there.

Anita had been a lonely young woman ever since she came from England. Maude saw that and often times she wished a nice young man could have been around to keep her company. Surely not John, whom she had observed fishing around and trying to take advantage of her vulnerability.

Maude hated his guts. He was so sloppy, audacious and

heartless. She couldn't stand the sight of him and tried not to get in his way. Anita's father, by now, must have suspected something could be going on, but being such a busy man Maude wondered if he had time to notice anything.

Jerome was all that Maude had been living for. She had no kids of her own, and was more than happy to take care of him when his mother passed away. She had watched him develop into a very intelligent and articulate young man who could have a bright future were it not for slavery. Many nights she prayed to Massa God and Jesus Christ for their freedom and for her to live long enough to see slavery abolished.

Maude was fifty-five years old; a very strong woman from her appearance. Medium built, her firm legs and broad shoulders gave her the characteristics of a hard worker. And that she was. She had charm too. Alfred oftentimes listened to her African tales whenever he was resting in the living room, after a hard day's work. The stories were colourful folk tales, full of myth, mirth and magic, something Alfred was fond of. He liked to watch her dark brown, sparkling eyes, trying to convince him the stories could have been true.

Maude was also looking forward to the day when Jerome, a free man, would have a family and children. There were very few young women in his age group around, except for the nearby plantation which had about three or four. There was one particular young girl there, Alice Rowe, who had eyes for Jerome. He knew nothing of the sort. Maude was waiting for the right time to plant a spark between them. Now she wondered if someone else could be lurking in the shadows, ready to light a fire. She didn't know what to think, especially when it involved a white woman.

Maude finished her dinner: boiled yams, sweet potatoes, pumpkin and steamed, salted cod. It was her favourite and she looked forward to preparing it for everybody, more so the men, who worked so hard during the day. Jerome liked that too.

Maude had been watching him all evening. He seemed pretty quiet, reserved and probably tired. At one point Babwe came over to him and whispered in his ear. He laughed and then became deep in thought. Most of the other slaves had finished eating and one by one they disappeared to their little cosy spot to get a good night's rest. Except for storytelling nights, Saturday, and sometimes Fridays, it was early to bed and early to rise.

'Aren't you going to bed, Mama?' asked Jerome, as he came over to sit beside her. 'Everyone seemed tired tonight.'

'You are not tired?'

'Sure. I was about to go myself, but I thought I would help you clean up. It must be a long day for you at the house there and then here.'

'Not really – Mrs Elsie and Doris did most of the cooking today.' They were both cooks who prepared meals for the slaves, whereas Maude cooked for Alfred and Anita and all the foremen.

'You must be tired though after having to sleep out there last night,' Maude looked him straight in the eyes, wanting to get a reaction.

'I was so tired I fell asleep right away.'

'You are lucky it didn't rain... and the mosquitoes.'

'I am. Anyway Mama, I will be going; see you in the morning.'

'Good night son. I hope you sleep better tonight.'

'I hope so too.'

Nothing unusual, Maude thought. Probably it was just her imagination and overreaction.

★

Anita must have dozed off. As soon as Alfred opened the front door she jumped out of her slumber.

'Hey, you didn't sleep well last night honey?' Alfred said wearily, resting his leather bag on the couch.

'What time is it? It's dark already,' she said with a yawn.

'It's only eight o'clock dear but if you are tired go and get some rest.'

'I should but I have been waiting up for you.'

'Why?'

'There's something I want to say to you.'

'Go on.'

'Mom will be coming in another few months.'

'Right.'

'Don't you think we should start preparing?'

'Hmmnn. I guess you are right. But how?' The thought of Lynda relieved his tiredness and he was happy the subject came up. Alfred had been thinking about her so much in the past few weeks and it was good to share his thoughts about her.

'I was thinking of getting some new furniture, decorations...'

'But where would you get that?' he questioned.

'I can take the buggy to Malvern and get them.'

'Malvern? That far?'

'I will take Maude and a couple of the men with me.'

'You sure you will be okay?'

'C'mon Dad, with them everything will be all right.'

'When will you go?'

'On Saturday, or we leave Friday morning and come back on Saturday night.'

'What about the dance on Saturday?'

Anita was surprised he remembered that. 'Oh! You remember that? How did you know I was going?'

'John asked me,' he said without even smiling.

'John?'

'I suspect you two have become good friends, or is it something else?'

'Dad, what did he tell you?' A little anger built up in her voice.

'Nothing,' he said, looking at her. 'He just wanted to ask me if I would allow you to go to the dance with him.'

'And?'

'I told him you are a big woman now and that it is something for you to decide on. Nevertheless, I told him it was okay with me.'

She smiled. 'Dad, John and I are getting to know each other, that's all. I wouldn't mind going to the dance with him, as it will help relieve the boredom here, but my priority right now is Mother's coming. If I get back in time on Saturday and I am not tired then I will go with him. If not, I will just go to bed early.'

'I see. I was only concerned about you being tired and all that.'

'Don't worry, I will be okay,' she smiled.

'You must be really looking forward to Lynda's coming.'

'You know what you are talking about. I can hardly wait; how about you?'

'Honey, I have to admit that I have been really missing her, especially since you arrived. I need her more than ever now.'

'She will soon be here, Dad. I know you must really miss her, but don't worry, everything will be all right.'

*

Maude had just finished washing the dishes when Anita walked in, stretching her arms in a show of sleepiness.

'You didn't sleep well last night?' Maude asked, with hands akimbo like she was giving an order. Sometimes Maude played the role of mother, something which Anita didn't mind. At least she felt cared for. It was one of the reasons why she had a soft heart for those poor slaves, who apparently had no one to stand up for them.

'Oh, Maude, I feel like going right back to bed.'

'Well young miss, you do that. You went partying last night?'

'Partying? I was up thinking.'

'About?'

'About Mom… Dad.'

'That's nice.'

'I can hardly wait for Mom to be here. By the way, I have to go to Malvern on Friday and I need you to come along with me.'

Maude giggled. She always liked to go to Malvern. It was such a welcome break from Big Yard. 'Oh sure. We two?'

'No, Babwe will be coming too and I am thinking of taking another young slave.'

'Who?' she asked quickly, hoping to hear the name she suspected.

'I don't know yet. I will have to decide by this evening.'

'Oh.'

'It's getting too dangerous out there – Dad thinks I need all the protection I can get, so I think it best to take a younger person with us.'

'I couldn't agree more,' Maude said, a little disappointed at not hearing the name.

★

Anita watched the tired, weary and hungry-looking slaves come up the path alongside the back porch of the house, after a hard day's work. Most of them passed like they had not seen her. It was a pity they didn't realise how much concern she had in her heart for their welfare. She surveyed them, her eyes searching for a young one she had only seen once – and at night. Her heart raced when her eyes darted to the back of the line and did not recognised anyone looking like him. She saw Babwe, recognising him instantly. Babwe had gone to Malvern with her on every trip so far. He was a good talking partner, not to mention his storytelling skills. Maude and Babwe were very talented in that area.

'Hi missus,' said Babwe as he was about to pass her. 'Howdy.'

'Hi Babwe. You look tired.'

'That's my life story, ma'am.'

'Smile, because you will get a break on Friday.'

'Malvern?' he almost laughed.

'How did you know?'

'I just guessed.' Jerome had walked up behind Babwe and was about to pass them both when Anita stopped him.

'Hi, I need your help.'

Jerome looked behind him, anticipating that she might have been speaking with someone else. There was no one else around.

'Yes ma'am,' he mumbled.

'I have to go to Malvern on Friday, and I need you and Babwe to come along with me.'

'Yes ma'am.'

'I thought I'd let you know before time so you can be prepared.'

'Yes ma'am. Thank you.' Babwe looked at him with a smile of triumph and promise.

'I will see you on Friday then,' she said and disappeared around the corner of the house. John was only a few yards down the pathway, but could not have seen her talking with them. A clump of overgrown crotons would have blocked his view.

As soon as she had left, Babwe nudged Jerome in the side.

'See, she likes you,' he teased.

'Don't get me into any trouble,' Jerome murmured.

'We'll see. Only time will tell, my son.'

Jerome didn't want to continue the conversation. He didn't want to build up his hopes and then be popped like a balloon. He knew Maude would be going with her as she and Babwe always did. The journey should be interesting. He had never gone to Malvern, hence the impending visit should be more than an experience.

Notwithstanding all of that, he was faced with the question he didn't want to ask himself because he feared what the answer might turn out to be. Why was the young woman doing all this for him? She probably didn't even know his name. Maybe Babwe was right. She was up to something. But how could she, when on more than one occasion he had seen her and John walking and talking in a kind of romantic way?

As far as Jerome was concerned, the penalty for loving a white woman was death. To society it didn't matter whether the woman loved a slave; what mattered was when the slave returned that love. He could easily forget her if it ever came to the test wherein he had to make a choice, he thought. But then again, he might just be dreaming. All of this so far could be one grand illusion which was as far from reality, as far as the moon was from the sun.

The Malvern trip, he thought, should shed more light on the puzzle, if there was any at all. If she had chosen him for the Malvern trip deliberately, and with reason, then he might have an idea what the attractive and gorgeous daughter of his slave master was up to.

Wednesday and Thursday Jerome worked hard as usual, trying to take his mind off the planned trip to Malvern. He tried to think as little as possible about Anita and what she might have been up to. Babwe gave him a good outline of what to expect on the trip. He would feel a little freedom from home; the burning sun would give him a kind of short break, the food was a change, but worst of all they sometimes had to sleep under the buggy. The latter he didn't mind because he had company – good company.

The days went by quickly and Friday morning came with much anxiety for Jerome. He was up around five thirty; but Babwe had beaten him to it. Jerome was taken aback when he slipped into the kitchen to find him sipping hot, black coffee from a huge and rusty-looking mug. A sweet potato roasted on coal was the accompaniment. Usually the potato is roasted overnight and left in the ashes to keep warm until daybreak, depending on the size of the fire: most times it had a little warmth, thus making it much softer to bite. Babwe was getting on in age and so too were some of his teeth, which were ruined by tobacco stains. He liked it when the potato was warm.

'Huh, you are up already?' a yawning Jerome blurted out, breaking the silence of the quiet morning.

Babwe looked up, a lousy grin jerking his face. 'Hi, muh boy. You are ready?'

'I-I think so.'

'Come here... take this potato and grab a cup over there because you need something solid in your stomach for this long journey.'

'Aunt Maude is sleeping?'

'Yeah but she will soon be up. I like early mornings like this when I can relax and don't have to think about going in the field.'

Within a few minutes Maude came into the dimly-lit room, rubbing her eyes. 'I can see you all are ready,' she said wearily. 'I feel like I haven't slept at all.'

'You look it Maude, you look as if sleep was far away from you last night,' said Babwe.

Jerome wasn't following the conversation; he was more interested in the potato.

'That potato must be really good,' said Maude. The comment still didn't register, 'Jerome... good morning.'

There was silence for about fifteen seconds.

'Huh... eh... Oh! Morning Aunt Maude. Are you ready?'

'Yes I am. That potato must be really good.'

'It surely is. I don't know where Babwe grew this one.'

'Right where the others came from,' he grinned, to-bacco-stained teeth faintly visible in the almost dark kitchen.

'Anyway guys, I will just grab my coffee and then we are ready. Babwe, how about the horses and the buggy?'

'Ready and waiting.' The first thing Babwe did when he woke up earlier was to check on them.

Outside, it remained dark. However, a faint glow in the eastern sky indicated that a new day was dawning. The rooster had already given his signal twice.

It was time to go. Jerome was gripped with anxiety. As he walked towards the buggy he looked over his shoulder at the other slave quarters with tears in his eyes. He could hear the movements of pots and pans, plates and spoons, as they gulped down the usual – porridge – most likely cornmeal, in preparation for another day of hard work. He was happy to be going away from it all and he wished it was permanent, but somehow he felt bad that so many of his brothers and sisters had to endure another day of it. Luckily for him, he got a reprieve.

'Are you sad you are going?' a soft voice said, interrupting his thoughts. Anita stood right in front of him with two bags in her hand.

Jerome wasn't certain what to say so he grabbed both bags from her just in time to see Babwe pull up in the buggy.

'Thank you. Are you all ready?' she asked.

'Sure am ready ma'am,' said Maude. 'An early start is

always good.'

Jerome put down the bags quickly in order to help Anita up into the buggy. Babwe saw the outstretched hand and could have helped her from his vantage point but thought that probably that hand was meant for Jerome. He felt relieved that Jerome took it.

Anita walked up close to him. He could smell the fragrance of her perfume in the cool, fresh, morning air. He was nervous and were it not for the absence of light, Anita could have seen the trembling hands. Her warm hand came into his and held it tightly. Somehow, as she was about to place her foot on the first step of the buggy she slipped, losing her balance, and in the end falling straight into Jerome's waiting arms. Nervous or not, Jerome realised he had to hold her; whether it was deliberate or simply an accident, he could not afford to let her fall to the ground. He felt the full weight of her body blending into his broad chest. Her protruding breasts squeezed against his body, and it was at that moment doubt came into Jerome's mind about the authenticity of the fall. She remained in his arms for a good five seconds before she felt Jerome starting to withdraw.

'Oh! My... that was so clumsy. I could have hurt myself,' she said, a smile rippling across her face. 'Thank you so much er...'

'Jerome. Jerome Scott,' he said, smiling too.

'That's my boy,' said Maude, grinning at his triumph over preventing Anita from falling.

'Our boy,' interjected Babwe; again, a loud laugh accompanying his grin.

'It's a sign that everything will go well on this journey,' said Anita, getting back her composure.

They took up their positions on the buggy. Babwe held the reins, Jerome was beside him, while Anita and Maude were in the back seat. It was a cute little buggy with all the necessary features such as a covering in the event of rain, and extra blankets should there be a need to sleep on the journey or overnight. There were also extra supplies of cured ham, salted beef, beans, coffee, biscuits, bread, oranges, bananas, avocado, and sugar.

'We seem to be all ready.'

'Yes ma'am, but where's Massa Campbell? Is he going to see us off?'

'He was sleeping and I did not want to wake him because he had a late night last night,' remarked Anita.

'Oh! But you know he's always here whenever we have to leave,' said Babwe. She was about to come down from the buggy when Alfred emerged from the shadows.

'I was just wondering if you had all gone,' he said.

'I didn't want to wake you, Dad.'

'That's all right. Who have we here now?' he said, coming up closer to the buggy.

'Maude and...'

'Jerome, sir, Jerome Scott.'

'Oh! Jerome, I remember you. Anita, are you making the right choice here?'

'C'mon Dad, I don't think there will be a problem.'

'You probably weren't aware that only this week he was sent to Hell House for punishment.'

Jerome stared at the ground; Babwe looked away and Maude stared at Alfred.

Anita looked at her father straight in the eyes. 'Whatever he was punished for, Dad, has nothing to do with this assignment. I have a gut feeling that he might be the best addition for the journey and I am willing to take a chance on that.'

Alfred was surprised. 'We are talking about your security.'

'Trust me on this one Dad.'

'I know Babwe and Maude will do well, but I am not

certain about this man. He has been to Hell House twice.'

'That doesn't say much, Dad. Everyone deserves a second chance. Just a few minutes ago I could have injured myself if it weren't for Jerome.'

'What happened?'

'I was about to climb the buggy when I slipped and he caught me just in time.'

'All right, you win this time.' Alfred bent over and kissed her on the cheek. 'Have a good trip and you all take good care of her,' he said, beckoning to them.

'Yes sir,' said Babwe. 'We guarantee you that.'

'Good. See you all tomorrow.'

'Bye Dad.'

The buggy sped off into the morning. Anita looked back into the dark. Another figure came running towards Alfred who gazed after them. Anita was certain it was John. She was happy he wasn't there to see her off. She smiled to herself. She had won round one.

Chapter Four

The buggy moved further and further away from the miseries and agonies of Big Yard. A day away from the plantation was a blessing in disguise for Babwe, Maude, and now Jerome. Anita – to her it was just fun. In essence, she didn't really have to go on a trip like that. Nevertheless, she capitalised on her father's loneliness and yearning for her mother and took the opportunity she had been hoping for all along, i.e. to have some time with the young slave; to get to know Jerome better, and without any restrictions, was all that was on her mind right now.

The first two miles of the journey were almost in silence. It was a little dark but soon that huge orange ball of fire known as the sun would creep over the Spur Tree Hills to the east of them, and spread its golden rays on their jerking bodies. The horses came to a slow trot at the command of Babwe.

'What's the matter?' asked Anita.

'Thought I'd just give the horses a five minute break if that's okay with you ma'am.'

'Oh, that's all right.'

The horses had stopped in their tracks, their heads already lowered to the dew-covered grass overflowing into the narrow road. The quiet morning gave way to the sound of gushing water from a small stream bordering the road. The horses didn't seem interested in the sound of the water; the thick mound of fresh, green grass was more to their liking.

Jerome stepped down from the buggy, the moment the horses came to a halt. He joined Babwe in holding the reins to allow them to feed. Maude was slumped down in a rather comfortable position. Jerome saw Anita trying to make her way down from the buggy and rushed to help her.

'Here,' he said extending his hand, 'let me help you ma'am.'

'Oh, thanks. How nice of you.'

'You are most welcome, ma'am.'

Anita looked at him, leaning her head to one side. 'You know, you seem to be a nice person...'

Jerome turned away his head and was about ready to walk back towards Babwe.

'Jerome! Please wait.' Jerome turned around to meet her gaze. 'I know it's a bit awkward, you being a slave and I being the slave master's daughter, but I would like to get to know you better. Can we be friends?'

'Ah... I...'

'It's okay Jerome. I know you are shy; but please, take your time, no rush. Can we be friends?'

'Y-yes... N-no ma'am. I...'

'I tell you what. Let it be our secret, Jerome. No one will know except you and me. Is that okay?'

Jerome nodded in the affirmative. 'I h-have to be careful ma'am. You know that is trouble.'

'Yes I know Jerome and that is why it must be our little secret, right?'

'Right, ma'am.'

'Okay, go back to Babwe now and always remember our secret.'

Anita watched with lustful eyes as he walked away from her. She felt triumphant; she felt victorious. She had found a treasure and that was her little secret.

Maude smiled with half-closed eyes. She didn't fully

open them until she was certain Anita had moved away from the buggy and was walking towards the stream. So that was it! Their little secret was no longer one. Maude had heard everything and her suspicions all along had now been proven right. Anita was up to something; it could mean trouble, real trouble for Jerome, and at that point, Maude was not convinced that she should get involved. She had had more than one conversation with Alice Rowe, who seemed very much in love with Jerome. In fact, Maude had promised to arrange for both of them to meet one Sunday at church. She had hoped for a meeting soon but she had been so tired recently that she didn't get around to doing it. She, too, would have to keep her mouth shut regarding the impending developments. Suppose John ever had knowledge of what had just transpired? She hated to think of the consequences.

'It's so nice out here,' Babwe said to Jerome as he approached him.

'Yea, it would even be nicer if we were free.'

'Free? Oh my boy, I don't know if that will be a possibility in my lifetime.'

'Sure it will. The news from the east gets more encouraging all the time.'

'We need to pray more, my son.'

'I guess you are right.'

'Is Miss Anita okay?'

'Yes. She is over there,' he said, pointing behind a clump of bushes.

'She is one of the more kind-hearted ones. I like these trips because she treats us like human beings. I am glad you could come to get a taste of freedom.'

'Hmmnn, I am looking forward to it.'

'You will enjoy it, I can assure you. You have to be grateful to Miss Anita. Do as she says and you will be chosen again to come back.'

'You think so?'

'Certainly. I have been coming with her for quite a while. This is my eighth time and I enjoy every one of them.'

'That sounds encouraging.'

'Encouraging it is my boy. She seems to like you Jerome and, if she does, you can bet you will be here again, probably two or three times before Christmas.'

Anita came up towards them. 'They are having a field day,' she said, referring to the horses.

'Oh yes ma'am, they just love the fresh grass. The dew makes it nicer and that's why they couldn't care less about the water.'

'Will you soon be ready?'

'I am right now, ma'am.'

She turned to go up the steps of the buggy, Jerome moving swiftly again to help her. He felt the squeeze of her hand as she placed it into his grip to enable her to climb without falling. But even after she was seated she took her time in releasing her hand. Jerome didn't look her in the eye but pretended that the touch meant nothing. Maude watched from the corner of her eyes; her heart pounded with either rage or joy. She wished she knew which one it was. Babwe watched the scenario and he too felt that the grip was much more than normal. Like Maude, he too wasn't certain whether to support what could eventually blossom into a forbidden love affair.

The journey resumed and for the most part, the next three miles were covered in silence. The journey was often bumpy; and there were times when Anita felt nauseous and so sick in the stomach that she wanted to vomit. When she couldn't take it any longer she mumbled to Babwe that she wanted to stop. Maude knew something was wrong.

'Don't push it Miss Anita. Let's take a little break.'

'My stomach is turning,' she said.

Jerome glanced behind him and saw the flushed face of Anita hanging low. He darted from his seat as soon as the buggy came to a halt and went around to the side where Anita was sitting. She looked up when he approached.

'I will be all right,' she told him.

'Come and get some fresh air over there,' he said, pointing to a huge oak tree just a step away from the side of the road.

'You sure you are not hungry?' asked Maude.

'I wouldn't mind eating something but give me a few minutes to settle down.'

The air was really refreshing. The surroundings were all green; no houses, plantations, or any other sign of human activity were in sight. The road was lonely too. A sign that they had passed about a half-a-mile up the road said Potsdam. Apparently, there was a plantation to the north of them. Some buggy tracks branched off at two spots a few yards before the place where they had stopped.

Babwe steered the buggy under the tree to a spot where the grass was not that tall. Jerome followed, his eyes watching the wheels to ensure that they did not get stuck in a hole or stumble on a rock. Eyes were also watching him; something he was unaware of at that moment. It was easy for Anita to hold up her head and from that angle, stare right into the eyes of Jerome. And she did just that. She watched him closely, her stomach ailment almost forgotten. Here was a young slave, she was convinced, who would give her life more meaning. She knew that from the very first night she saw him; yet she was reluctant to believe that at first, primarily because of their distinct classes of people.

It was forbidden love. But it could be a great love. It was something she could not rush into because she wanted to be absolutely certain that it was true and that it was not infatuation. On the other hand, Jerome's feelings were not known. He was shy and that was a bridge she would have to cross with him. It could take time.

The plantation was not the perfect place for a forbidden love to flourish. There was her father, John, slaves, and very soon, her mother. And what about Maude? Would she have her support? What about Babwe? They were probably the only two people she could rely on for that, hence her reason for taking them with her.

The buggy stopped and so did Jerome. As soon as he lifted up his head his eyes met Anita's and remained there for a few seconds. His gaze shifted to Maude, who looked at him with no expression on her fat and round face. Anita saw him, blushed and smiled.

'You are okay Jerome?' she asked him.

'Oh, I am fine ma'am, really fine. You will soon be fine too as soon as your stomach settles from the bumpy ride.'

'Let's get something to eat – it's past noon,' said Maude looking into the sky, as the midday sun shone in all its glory.

Maude grabbed a big bag from the buggy and an odour followed it that caught Babwe's sense of smell.

'What smells so nice?'

Maude grinned sheepishly. 'I have roast potato, cheese sandwiches, fried johnny cake, boiled eggs, fried plantain, and corned beef – that's for lunch. For dinner you have to wait until we get to Malvern.'

'Well, let's get the food rolling.'

They all sat down to a hearty meal. Within twenty minutes, the food disappeared into the empty stomachs. Even Anita ate ravenously. After the meal they relaxed for a while, absorbing the coolness of the tree before they undertook the final leg of the trip. If they travelled at the same pace as they had all morning they should be in Malvern by nightfall.

Jerome was the first to rise from his comfortable position. He went towards the horses. He wanted to ensure that they too were well taken care of before they resumed the journey. They should have had enough water when they made the first stop; now they had been busy eating ever since they had stopped. Jerome took a brush from under the buggy's seat and started smoothing the ruffled hair on their manes. They seemed to like it.

'That should feel really good.'

Jerome turned around in fright only to see Anita standing beside him with eyes all full of admiration for what he had been doing.

'Uh… I guess they like it ma'am.'

She came a little closer and said, almost in a whisper, 'I wish I had someone to relax me like that.'

Jerome pretended not to hear that comment. He felt rather awkward. What could he say anyway?

'There are times when I feel so tired that something like that would surely be good for me,' she smiled. Again, Jerome found it embarrassing, or rather undiplomatic, to comment.

'Wouldn't you like to do that for me sometime, Jerome?'

Again, he could not answer.

'Deep down I know you want to but are afraid to, or you are afraid of the consequences. Isn't that right Jerome?'

He looked at her. She knew he wanted to say something but was afraid of doing so.

'C'mon Jerome, say something.'

Nothing. Anita wanted to continue the monologue. Jerome could easily break it, she sensed. But there could be some negative consequences, should she continue to press him. She could get answers she didn't want to hear.

Maude watched them from the corner of her eye. She observed the expressions on both faces because their voices were kept low. In fact, Jerome wasn't really saying anything. She wondered why. She decided to walk over to where they were in the event that she could even catch a piece of the conversation.

Anita didn't see Maude coming. She approached from behind. Not even the heavy thud of her shoes on the thick grass caught the attention of Anita. Her thoughts were still on Jerome.

'...one day you will say something,' Anita said, turning around to go and in the process meeting face to face with Maude.

'Uh, I didn't hear you coming,' she mumbled. 'Are you ready?'

'Yes ma'am. If we leave now we should be there before nightfall.'

'Okay, we'd better go then, Jerome.'

The horses raced away into the afternoon haze of cloudy skies and shadowy trees. Having refreshed themselves, they bolted into the unknown with renewed vigour and enthusiasm. Their hooves pounded on solid ground, breaking the silence of the deep forest.

Jerome's silence was voluntary. He wanted time to think and the journey provided that. Babwe was occupied with controlling the speed of the horses and moreover, he seemed to be enjoying every moment of it.

There was no doubt about it. No doubt at all. Jerome was certain that Anita was serious about him. From all indications, she had no plans to give up. What could he do? A poor slave and a rich, white woman. He could count on the support of none, except for Babwe, probably. And he was not even certain about that either. Anita's father would be outraged, not to mention foreman John. Jerome trembled at the possible repercussions. What was it he was getting himself into? There could be an easy solution, he thought. Forget the whole thing and try to refuse her covert advances.

The next five miles were completed without any stops. Malvern was coming into view. Huge plantations, cultivation, and even a buggy or two going in all directions, were now common sights. Many slaves were around too moving like zombies at the command of overpowering forces.

The sun was dipping behind the Santa Cruz mountain range, which stretched into the Pedro Plains far below, Malvern would be a little cool during the night. There was a little easterly wind blowing across the town, a welcome relief following a scorching and humid day.

The wind caressed Anita's face teasingly. She gave in to it. She smiled. Tonight would be rather cool. She could do with some company; someone came to mind, and she smiled again.

Chapter Five

Malvern was a dusty, old, weather-beaten town. A stable, an inn, two general stores, a blacksmith's shop, a bar and a roofless market were all that formed Main Street. Nevertheless, it seemed to be a busy town.

It could have been described as a haven for buggies and horses. They moved up and down Main Street with masters and slaves busy gathering supplies for the weekend, and for the more privileged, or the pleasure seeker, a stop at the bar was a well-deserved reward following a week's hard work.

The town was perched on a plateau. Malvern was situated near to the highest point of the Santa Cruz mountain range. Its highest peak was less than five miles south of Malvern at a village called Potsdam.

Anita and her crew joined the throng on Main Street. Their first order of business would be to secure a room at the inn. On most occasions Anita asked Maude to share a room with her. That was not the norm; slaves were usually housed in their own quarters at a run-down shack at the back of the inn. But being the liberal-minded daughter of a plantation owner, it was no surprise Anita wanted Maude to stay with her.

The sun was slowly descending. Very soon, darkness would engulf the entirety of the surroundings. Babwe drew the buggy to a halt right in front of the inn. The smell of cornbread permeated the atmosphere, teasing growling stomachs and parched lips.

Maude was certain her eyes were fooling her. She

peered at the object again from one corner in order to get the right focus. The object came closer as they all alighted from the buggy.

'Hi Aunt Maude,' said the person who Maude had been trying to focus on.

'A-Alice... w-what... I didn't expect you here,' Maude mumbled.

'We came in earlier today and will be leaving early morning.'

'Oh! It is so nice to see I you. By the way, you know Babwe already. This is Anita, Mr Campbell's daughter and of course, you have met Jerome before.'

'You two know each other?' asked Anita.

'W-well yes,' said Jerome, uncertain whether he should have said that.

Alice was a beautiful, young, black slave girl. Her curvaceous body was faintly visible under the thick cotton skirt that she wore. Her wide lips were inviting, yet they could easily block any uninvited guest. The dark eyes carried a different picture; they could glow in friendliness but could also squint in anger.

Those eyes of Alice measured Anita from head to foot. She saw the look on Anita's face when she asked the question. A command was in the question; was she observing right? She had often thought about Jerome but was never convinced the right opportunity would present itself anywhere in the near future. Could it be now? Maude was her good friend, but why hadn't she made her feelings known to the woman Jerome regarded as his mother?

'Well, I am starving, so I suggest we get something to eat,' said Anita. 'It was nice meeting you Alice,' she said, turning towards the entrance of the inn. The others followed but not before Alice whispered in Maude's ear, 'I like him.'

Maude almost laughed aloud. Anita turned in her tracks

but not in time to see Alice withdrawing from her bent position.

'Come, let us go,' Anita said.

Jerome looked at Alice, not knowing what could have made Maude so happy. He hadn't thought of Alice any more than he had thought of Anita. In fact, Alice could make a good sister for her, he concluded. Alice passed him, deliberately bumping into his side without even uttering a word. Babwe watched her heading towards the general store, her hips making an undulating motion.

'She's growing into a nice young woman,' said Babwe.

Jerome looked at him with a smile. 'You know you are right. I have not been seeing much of her but she's turning out to be one fine young woman.'

'Don't talk too loud.'

'Why?'

'Hmmmm, Miss Anita may hear what she does not want to hear.'

Jerome's smile vanished from his face. He seemed to stumble when he took a step backward to lean against a lamp post in front of the store. 'Have you been observing?'

'Sure I have.'

'I don't know what to do, Babwe. She is coming on strong, too strong.'

'I saw her moves when we stopped.'

'Do you think Aunt Maude suspects something?'

'I don't know. She hasn't said anything.'

'I don't want to tell her but if she knows already then I wouldn't mind getting some advice from her.'

'But you don't want to tell her when in fact you could have avoided her knowing?'

'Exactly!'

'But sooner or later she will know.'

'Only if it lasts.'

'You don't expect it to?'

'No.'

'Why?'

'I don't think it will work – her father... John... the community, you know what I mean.'

'I understand son. You have to be very careful.'

'I cannot be too careful.'

'On the other hand, we could all be free men soon. Think about that too. When we are free we will be able to do things we aren't capable of doing now.'

'To give your love to a white woman in this kind of system is no bed of roses.'

'Look at it this way Jerome, it could mean many things for you – money for one.'

'Massa Campbell will never accept our relationship.'

'Hey, fellows, come and get something to eat,' shouted Anita, from the entrance to the inn.

'We will be there in a second,' said Babwe, grinning sheepishly. He led Jerome around to the back of the building where slaves normally eat. Within minutes they were devouring a sumptuous meal of cornbread, beef stew, potatoes and hot chocolate.

After the meal they took the buggy around to the sleeping quarters where it would be visible to them. By the time they had finished taking care of the horses, feeding and watering them, it was pitch black – completely dark. The stars were peeping out; the evening star, Venus, was already glittering away. Tonight would have been good for story-telling but everyone was too tired to do so.

Babwe walked over to the slave sleeping quarters and sat on a section of the front porch, where he would have a full view of the stars. A portion of the town could also be seen from that angle. Jerome, deep in thought, followed. He, too, took a seat on the porch. Somehow, tonight reminded him of the last time he slept at Hell House.

As soon as his thoughts raced to Anita, there she was

standing before the two of them. She had changed into fresh clothes; her hair was neatly combed and, overall, she seemed rested. The back was poorly lit. The only source of light came from a couple of windows at the back of the inn. A lamp post from Main Street shone feebly into the inn's backyard. Not surprisingly, that didn't stop Jerome from detecting the faint smile on her white face.

'Are you all right? Did you have enough to eat?'

'Oh yes, Miss Anita; it was sure nice too. Thank you ma'am.'

'That's okay. Jerome, I was wondering if you could empty my bath for me.'

'Sure ma'am,' he said, getting up almost immediately.

'I will soon be back, Babwe.'

'If you don't see me out here I am gone to get a nap.'

'You need the rest, Babwe. Good night,' said Anita.

'Maude is sound asleep already.'

'She needs the rest – getting old like me,' he grinned.

They disappeared into the blackness of the night, their shadows fading out with the dullness of the light.

Bath? thought Babwe, as he got up from his rather comfortable seat, where he had only been sitting for a few minutes. Wasn't the inn responsible for getting rid of the bathwater? Funny, she was up to something. How could she when Maude was around? No! she was fast asleep, she had said. Watch out Jerome, here she comes! he uttered to himself.

Anita knew a slave could not be seen entering her room. She was smarter than that. There was a back door to her room, if she climbed up the wooden stairs. But neither would she chance that.

She was ahead of Jerome; as soon as they were a few steps from the stairs Anita spun around unexpectedly and rushed into the strong and sturdy arms of the young slave. He lost his balance; however, he regained his composure to welcome the slim, soft and warm body into his arms. Before he could take any action, whether defensive or offensive or even get to mutter something, a pair of warm lips crushed tightly against his. Jerome had never kissed a woman in his life, so he allowed her to have her way in this new experience.

She squeezed her body against his even tighter, while her lips and tongue searched his mouth, wiggling in and out, like the world was about to end. It didn't take long for Jerome to learn to reciprocate her moves and within a few seconds she started to moan, groan, and sigh with forbidden pleasure. They held each other for about five minutes, Jerome being the first to let go. Even when he accomplished that she came close again, placing her head against his stomach.

'Are you mad at me?' she mumbled.

'Maybe, maybe not.'

'I have been wanting to do that from the very first night I saw you. It had to happen, sooner or later. I can't resist you.'

'Of course, you know this means trouble.'

'I love you Jerome,' she said, withdrawing in order to look into his face in the dark. 'I am willing to face the consequences, although I know you could be in more trouble than I.'

'That's it. I could be the one in hot water. You are a free woman and I am a slave.'

'You could be free soon, too,' she said, relief in her voice. 'The reports I am getting suggest this could happen much sooner than we think.'

'But the problem is what do we do in the meantime.'

'That is up to us,' she said, coming into his arms again.

Was this woman serious about what she had said? Was she acting responsibly? Her hide was covered because of the fact that she was white but as far as Jerome was concerned, he hardly had anyone to stand up for him in case of trouble. All his friends were slaves; could he take Anita seriously for a lover as well as a friend?

Chapter Six

Alice Rowe didn't feel like eating anything. In fact, she didn't have anything to eat all morning. She had come to Malvern with her mistress, Sarah Daniels, and an elderly slave, Charles. They hardly spoke; and that made matters worse for Alice.

Since they had left Malvern three hours ago, hardly anything had been said. Alice's thoughts drifted into a web of intricate possibilities regarding Jerome. She, too, had eyes for him but jealousy hadn't burned the walls of her stomach until she saw him today in the presence of another woman – a white one at that.

She had dreams of a wild and rocky relationship between Jerome and Anita; that was only last night. She woke from the dream and as soon as she had fallen asleep again, there was Jerome and Anita grinning at her mockingly. It was a nightmare of some sorts. Now, she was wide awake, yet the nightmare kept gnawing at her thoughts. She wished she had someone to talk to. Alice looked sideways at Sarah, an easygoing woman who, although not the talkative type, was pretty easy to get along with. At least, much easier than her husband Larry. Sarah was a petite blond woman with brown eyes and a heavily tanned face. She stood no more than about five feet two inches, and from all indications, she spent a lot of time outdoors. There were times when she found herself in the cane fields with Larry and the other slaves. She took his lunch there whenever there was little time for him to come home. Afterwards, she would remain there until late afternoon finding something constructive to do.

Sarah sensed when she saw that glance that Alice wanted to say something to her. 'Is everything okay?' she asked Alice. That was a favourite phrase for Sarah.

She treated her well, Alice had to admit. Sometimes she wondered whether she was truly a slave. Larry, too, might be rough on the men but when it came to Alice, it was like she was royalty.

For the other slaves and freemen on the Daniels' plantation, Alice was an eye-catcher. Sarah knew that and probably that was one of the reasons she treated her so well. There was no denying it, she told herself, Alice was a beautiful woman.

'I guess, sort of…'

'It looks like something is bothering you. You are not usually that quiet.'

'That's true.'

Sarah looked into the cobalt blue sky. 'I can remember how on other trips you chirped away while I listened with nothing much to say, only to admire your soft and poetic voice.'

Alice blushed. 'Have I been that entertaining?'

'Sure you have. I could listen to you all day, Alice, and I hoped sometimes that your parents were around to hear you.'

Alice didn't know her parents; they both died from tuberculosis when she was about four years old. She was now nineteen and had lived on the Daniels' plantation from the time of its first owner, Jacob, Larry's father. 'I wish I knew them. Sometimes I try so hard to remember anything at all but to no avail. You have been good to me Miss Sarah – you and Massa Daniels and I don't know how to thank you.'

'Soon, you could be a free woman, Alice, and we will miss you.'

Alice detected a crack in her voice and knew she was worried about that likelihood. 'That's a dream, Miss Sarah. I don't know if that will ever happen in my lifetime.'

'We have not been saying anything much Alice. Between us, it could be sooner than we could imagine.'

Alice looked at her again. She knew she meant what she had said. 'Really. What am I going to do?'

'Anything. You could leave us – find a young man and probably get married.'

'Married? You mean that?' Her thoughts raced to Jerome; once again they drifted into all kinds of possibilities.

'What is it that you are not telling me, Alice,' said Sarah, ready for a meaningful conversation about her thoughts.

'Hm a… I have some things on my mind but I am not certain if I should say them because they are not real.'

'What do you mean?'

'I…'

'Yes?'

'I-I… someone has been occupying my thoughts.'

'Just now, or is it something which has been going on for some time?'

'It's been going on for a while but ever since I left Malvern I seem to have been more preoccupied with it than at any other time.'

'Is it someone I know?'

'Maybe. No. I don't think so.'

'You can tell me. You don't have to worry.

'I don't have anyone anyway.'

Sarah reached across and squeezed her hand. 'Charles, pull up at the nearest suitable spot and let's eat.'

'That's a good idea,' said Alice.

★

Anita had been busy all morning, trying to secure all the things she came to get in Malvern. However, that didn't stop her from recollecting the memorable moments last night. She had finally gotten through to Jerome and oh... what a triumphant feeling. Jerome, along with Maude and Babwe, had been with her all morning getting the most vital goods they needed – flour, beans, ham, bacon, corn-meal, candles, matches, oil for the lamps, rice, salted cod, tea, coffee and biscuits. Luckily, the plantation was self-sufficient in sugar, eggs, milk, butter, chicken, beef, mutton, red kidney beans, vegetables, potatoes, pumpkins and yams.

Jerome stayed close to Anita all morning, so close that there were a few occasions when Jerome could smell her minty-fresh breath. Anita liked his closeness; she wished he could be that near all the time.

Maude was convinced now that her actions meant more than friendship. She observed the smiles, the glow on her face whenever Jerome was around, and most of all those tempting gesticulations.

It was Babwe who didn't have to be convinced that a spark had been ignited between the two. He had suspected all along, and now he had the confirmation of what had happened last night. Jerome told him everything and while he feared the consequences, he couldn't dwell on that negative aspect. Babwe's advice to Jerome: don't push anything, let things happen in their own time and place. It was advice that had been given to him so many times by his 'father' and he deemed it appropriate to pass it on to his 'son' Jerome.

Jerome and Babwe took the supplies to the buggy and packed them so as to allow space for what was left to come. Jerome left Babwe at the buggy and was on his way back to the General Store when he met Maude coming with some of the purchases.

'Are you all right?' Maude asked him, as she handed him the packages.

'Yes, Aunt Maude.'

'Did you see Alice anytime today?'

'No. Why?'

'I was wondering if she had left already. She didn't say when she was leaving – whether it was in the morning or the afternoon.'

'I guess she must have left already.'

'It seems so. Isn't she a nice girl?'

'Uh, sure. Sh-she is a nice girl.'

'She's always at church; she's that type – real nice and decent.'

'I have not been going to church, so that's why I haven't been seeing much of her.'

'You know church is the only meeting place or social life we have so we all should try to meet as often as possible.'

'That's so true. I must try to go to church more often.'

'I would like that. Alice would too,' she smiled.

'She would?'

'I am almost certain she would.'

Anita came up to join them with some more packages. 'Maude, can you fetch the rest of the things? I will take these.'

When Maude had left she turned to Jerome; it was the first moment they had had alone since last night.

'Can I buy you something?' she asked Jerome.

'You know that's not possible. I-I mean it is not practical or wise.'

Anita thought about it for a while. 'Okay, I think you are right. Are you okay?'

'I am.'

'Have you been thinking about last night?'

'W-well yes.'

'Any regrets?'

'W-well no.'

'You better not because I don't know when that opportunity will arise again.'

'You know, I never thought of that before.'

'I have and I realise I have to make use of every opportunity we have to be alone and I want you to think that way too, Jerome.'

'Okay, I will,' he said reluctantly, realising that he was opening up a little more to her, and even went as far as committing himself to finding ways that they could see each other back at the plantation.

'I wish I could stay one more night here. I won't come on a Friday again. Instead, I will come on a Thursday and stay two nights.'

Jerome looked at her in wonderment. 'What will you tell your father?'

'Oh, I will find some excuse. The only thing that might be a problem is my mother.'

'Your mother?'

'Yes. She is coming pretty soon.'

'Won't that complicate matters between us?'

'Not necessarily. That's why I said we both have to work on ways to see as much of each other as possible.'

Jerome paused, unsure of what exactly he should say. 'We will see,' he said.

'By the way, I have to get some clothes for Mom and as soon as we do that we have to leave.'

'Yes, we have to get going soon.'

'We will have to be on the road at night but that won't bother me.'

'Why?'

'It's a full moon, you will be with me, and I won't be able to go to the dance tonight with John.'

'You had promised to go with him?'

'He had asked me and I told him I'd try to be back before dark.'

'Are you two involved in some relationship or…'

Anita laughed, almost aloud. 'He thinks he is but I am not even sure. He's just a fat slob who keeps me company.'

'I don't like him at all.'

'Jerome, he could be dangerous too. I know he is going to be mad with me.'

'But didn't you say he kept your company sometimes?'

'Yes. He even wants to marry me.'

'Was it that serious then?'

'I wouldn't say serious. It's… it's kinda difficult to say. I want to be honest with you Jerome. Probably, he took it serious and I have been luring him indirectly into some kind of relationship, but all that has changed ever since I met you,' she said, looking at him. 'You are all I care about now and I couldn't care one bit about John. I only cared for him as a friend and good company, nothing else. I wish I could say that to him and clear up everything. It won't be that easy, Jerome. I don't know if it will ever be, even when you are a free man. That's the reality we have to live with right now.'

'I can see that.'

'Are you ready to face up to it, Jerome?'

'Probably, probably not.'

'If you have any feeling for me, you will, sooner or later.'

'At least you realise how difficult this is for me.'

'It's because I care about you and your concerns.'

'Thanks.'

She edged closer. Jerome looked around to see if anyone was looking.

'I would do anything for you, Jerome. In short, in a short space of time I have grown to love you more than anything else.'

'You have to promise me one thing, Anita.'

Her lips parted in anticipation of his request. 'Yes, anything... anything for you, Jerome.'

'No one, not even your mother, must know anything about us until I am a free man.'

'That's all?'

'Yes.'

'Well you won't have to worry about a thing.'

'That's comforting.'

'Let's hope one day we will be able to live openly with our love,' she smiled.

Chapter Seven

The days lingered through their strenuous tasks. The weeks seemed to be so unkind. There was little hope that there would be any improvement in the lives of slaves on the island. The abolition movement did pick up steam but forces were working against them. And that did have some effect.

Plantation owners drew closer when they saw the prospect of losing their precious commodity – slaves, staring them in the face. Meetings were held more frequently and owners were very much up to date on the latest developments. They were quite aware of the efforts of the now famous British anti-slave activist William Wilberforce; it was not something they could understand: a white man fighting to end the very system which had enabled them to become rich and powerful.

Anita had managed to squeeze a lot of information out of her father regarding the possible uprising. She feared what could happen to her father but at the same time, an uprising could be the answer to her problems. Jerome could be a free man and that was all that mattered to her.

Lynda was expected in two weeks and she wondered if her presence would change anything. John? She hadn't seen much of him since she refused to go to the dance with him. He had visited her the day after, and unintentionally Anita got angry with him and told him to forget everything. A red-faced John had stormed out of the house, vowing to himself to find out who was the man in her life. He had a gut feeling she had found someone else – probably in Malvern or even from the community. John felt humiliated and rejected, so much so that he rarely visited the house, unless he really wanted to speak with Alfred.

It was Sunday morning in Big Yard. Aunt Maude was getting ready for church. She felt triumphant. She had been able to convince Jerome and Babwe to come to church with her. They had agreed.

Church was an old abandoned storehouse on a nearby plantation. It was only attended by slaves and it was the only place they had an opportunity to meet as one. Many saw it as a chance to meet and made use of it.

The sermons were usually good and that seemed to be the only hope for them. Many were committed and faithful to God. The slave owners liked that. The missionaries who came from England did a good job of convincing them that Massa God was the true and only living God and that if they wanted to get to heaven, they had to live a life of obedience to their master and to God. As a result, many slaves were against any possible uprising; they felt it was evil and freedom could make life worse for them. Again, the owners liked that. It was a way to holding on to power over them.

Maude knew that Alice would be at church. Hence, the invitation to Jerome. Being fully convinced now that Anita wanted a relationship with Jerome, she thought if he was able to see Alice more often then Anita could be in trouble.

'Oh, it is so nice to see you all,' a smiling Alice said, as she greeted all three of them.

'Do you know how long we have been planning to come and keep putting it off?'

'Well, you are all here. Let's give Massa God thanks for that.'

'You are here every Sunday?' Babwe asked.

'Every Sunday. The church is my life and I wish more of

us could see it that way. Anyway, they are ready, let's go inside and we can talk afterwards.'

A young man, about thirty years old, introduced only as Pastor Bernie, gave an inspiring sermon about Jesus's shed blood and the need to have faith in him. The church was lively and emotional for most of the congregation. They sang, danced, clapped, cried, shouted for joy, and for once, forgot about their miserable lives. It was no surprise that there was such a turnout. Many came to seek some sort of solace, comfort, and a channel to soothe their fears and heal their wounds.

After the service, most of them remained and talked away, getting to know one another. Jerome managed to find himself alone with Alice soon after the intermingling started.

'So how have you been doing?' Alice asked.

Jerome looked around but didn't see Maude or Babwe. Looking at Alice a little bewildered, he said, 'I am fine, only a little tired.'

'Those long hours would kill anybody.'

'You know that is our life.'

'One day we will be free, whether in this life or the one to come.'

'I can see you have faith,' he said, looking more relaxed now.

'What more can I live for but God?'

'Well, you could look forward to abolition.'

'That is only a dream.'

'You think so?'

'I am convinced.'

'Well, a lot of things have been happening that you don't know about.'

'How do you know that?'

'I know.'

'How?'

'I have my sources.'

'Anita?'

'Anita? How does she come into all of this?'

'She figures somehow. Aren't you good friends?'

'We speak but only at the work level… only when it has something to do with work.'

'Are you certain about that?'

'Sure.'

'Hmmn. The way she looks at you suggests otherwise.'

Jerome was taken aback. She had been that observant? 'You are a woman of great detail. Did you notice that much about her?'

'It is not only her… I notice how you look at her too.'

'What? Are you suggesting that we have something going?'

A broad smile came across Alice's shining face. 'Here is a challenge Jerome. Are you ready for it?'

Jerome saw the boldness on her face and he was almost convinced that his guess was right. 'Go ahead,' he mumbled, rather nervously.

'If you don't have anything going with Anita, then can we see each other more often?'

Alice waited for his reaction. When it did come a few seconds after, she didn't know what he was thinking.

'That should not be a problem. We can see each other more often – every Sunday at least.'

Alice wanted to move closer. 'Would you want this anyway?'

'Of course I want to – who wouldn't want to keep company with a beautiful girl like you?' he smiled.

'We will see,' she blushed.

'Yes, we will see. Anita and I are just friends and that is how it will be. She is white and I am a slave. That's a big difference and that will remain for some time.'

'And if we were free?'

'That's an entirely different matter which I would not want to get into right now, but for the time being let's just see each other every Sunday. Right?'

'Right!' she laughed aloud.

Chapter Eight

Anita marched from one end of her room to the other, her shoes hit the wooden floor with a thud. She had been doing that for about two minutes when the burly looking figure of John stepped in, unannounced.

It was Friday afternoon. Anita had no real plans for the weekend. But as she watched the sun slumping down behind the horizon, she wished she could find some way to see Jerome over the weekend. She had not seen him all week; she was crazy, at least that was how she felt. If she did not see him by Sunday she could do something to blow their cover. She did not want that to happen but because of the way she felt about him, that meant little to her now. What could she do? She felt angrier now when she could not come up with a way out.

'A penny for your thoughts,' grinned John, closing the door behind him.

'Huh? Y-you startled me. I did not hear you come in.'

'Ah, I can do many things without being seen or heard,' he grinned again.

Anita felt her heartbeat race a little faster. Was he up to something? She would have to play the fool to catch the wise. 'You are everything eh?'

'Sure I am but that doesn't mean I don't get lonely sometimes.' The smile vanished from his red face.

'What are you trying to say, John?'

'A-Anita… I-I- think we should find some more time for each other.'

'Really?'

'I will have a little more time in the coming weeks as we get nearer to the end of the harvest and I was thinking maybe we could see each other a little more often.'

'Well, I don't know if—'

'If what?'

'If I will have the time, as I have to be preparing for Mom's coming.'

'That should not take long; you should have some time for yourself.'

'Dad wants me to ensure that everything is in order.'

'I am certain you are capable,' he laughed, almost aloud.

'I know that I am but...'

'Anita, you need to get out of the house. By the way, I was wondering if you would want to go to the Farmers' Market tomorrow.'

'Where?'

'In Junction.'

Junction was a small town about three miles away. Her mind skipped quickly from the room to Jerome.

'Okay, I will ask Maude to get a couple of slaves who can help us with the buggy and the things we are going to buy.'

'We don't need any slaves. I can manage,' he said, reassuringly.

Anita hated the idea of going with him alone. She had to beat him on that one. 'I feel safer when more people are around, what with word of a rebellion and all that sort of thing.'

'You have heard too,' he said, a little concerned.

'I have heard a lot. Dad is worried about me, I know, and I am certain he would feel more comfortable if we had some trustworthy slaves with us.'

'Do you really know of any slave you can trust?'

'Maude knows them and I can tell you whatever she says

I will go along with that.'

'As you say, ma'am. What time do you want to leave?'

'I would want to leave early and come back early.'

'That is fine with me, Anita,' he said coming a little closer. Without any notice, he pulled her into his arms and kissed her hard. Anita didn't resist him; she had to play the fool. Despite his tobacco-tainted breath, she had to endure his intrusion for a few seconds.

'I want you so much,' he said under his breath.

Anita didn't say anything, she was imagining Jerome in her arms. She thought that was the reason why she had been able to put up with the unwelcome gesture.

Anita woke earlier than usual. She hoped everything went as planned. She remembered the look on Maude's face when she told her she wanted Babwe and Jerome to go with her to Junction. She was puzzled by the look; it neither confirmed nor denied displeasure at the choice.

Maude had probably told them John would be going with her and she wondered how Jerome would react to that, given the altercation he had had with him a few weeks ago, when he was posted to Hell House. Her conclusion: Jerome wanted to see her as much as she wanted to see him. They wouldn't have an opportunity to even speak to each other but just seeing him would be enough, she thought.

Jerome didn't look at her when he and Babwe came around to the front of the house to meet John and Anita with the buggy. He deliberately tried to avoid her stare. Jerome felt anger. Anita could get him into deep trouble and he trembled at the thought. He wished he hadn't been chosen to come on the trip. It could turn out to be a disaster for him, simply because of the fact that his main enemy would be watching every move he made.

'Why are you taking this lazy bum? Couldn't you find someone much better?' he asked Anita. 'He is a troublemaker and a darn loser.'

'I don't know about you John, but he came with us to Malvern the other day and he was quite helpful. In fact, he performed exceptionally well.'

Jerome was relieved when he heard that. The moment the words were uttered from John's lips he heard that voice again, telling him to remain calm. Babwe boiled with anger too, but being a man getting on in age patience was one thing he had been able to exercise.

'Well, we will see my dear. Hell House is just waiting for him,' he grinned, the early morning drowsiness leaving his sour face. 'Okay boy, are you ready?' he asked Jerome.

'Yes, suh.'

'Good. Let's go. Remember, watch your step. If anything here should happen to m'lady God help your wretched soul, you hear me boy?'

'Y-yes, suh.'

'John what has gotten into you? Don't you see he knows what he is doing?'

'I hope to God you are right. I just don't trust him.'

'After today you will.'

John looked at her from the corner of his eyes. 'Never will,' he grumbled.

Anita looked at Jerome. She felt mad but had to constrain herself. She knew he was angry; he walked away to the back of the buggy like a dog with an injured tail. Anita hated that moment and wished he could put John in his rightful place.

Alfred emerged from the dark house in his pyjamas.

'Is everything okay out here?' he asked.

'Sure boss, everything is fine.' John had told him about taking Anita to Junction even before she did. He had promised to take care of her.

'I thought I heard some arguing out here.'

'I-I was only wondering if we had made the right choice

about the slaves we are taking.'

'I know Babwe, he is all right, and this young man I think was the one who went to Malvern the last time.'

'Yes Dad, and he did really well – no problems with him, for sure. He is obedient, works hard, and I felt really safe with a strong man around.'

John's face reddened but he remained silent.

'Well my dear, if you feel comfortable with him then that is fine with me. John, you are doing the right thing to make sure Anita gets the best. I appreciate that. Everything will be fine; you all go now and take care of yourselves.'

'Thank you sir,' said John.

'Anita, please try and find something nice for your mom – maybe a nice quilt or something.'

'I will Dad. Let's go then. See you Dad.'

'Take care my child and God be with you all.'

Three hours later the buggy rolled into Junction with four tired-looking people. They only stopped once on the way to water the horses and nothing much was said by either side.

Junction was a pretty small town. It had only one general store, a stable, small hotel, blacksmith shop, a bar, and a huge open lot where the action seemed to be at that time of morning – nine o'clock. The Farmers' Market was one huge mass of bonnets, bare heads and umbrellas. Primary and secondary colours dotted the huge open lot and everyone seemed busy as a bee. The buggy pulled up in front of the stable, the early morning sun glistening on the back of the horses. It was a beautiful day.

'Babwe, both of you take the horses to get water and feed and then wait for us right here.'

'Yes, suh.'

John held Anita by the hand and turned towards the gate of the market. Anita wanted to look back. However, she realised that would probably be unwise. She reluctantly followed John.

They shopped around for about two hours, picking up some food and home-made clothes as well as some freshly grown food such as yams and pumpkins, which they had little of back at the farm.

'John, could we get something to eat?' Anita asked, wanting to go back to where Jerome and Babwe were.

'Sure honey. We can go somewhere nice and have our lunch.'

'What about the boys?'

'Oh, I forgot about them. They can eat anything.'

'Where are they going to get it?'

'Didn't they bring lunch?'

'I don't know.'

'I can't help them if they didn't. I am sure you don't have enough for four.'

'I tell you what… here, buy fresh bread and some butter and milk over at that stall and let me ask them if they brought anything,' she said, pointing in front of her.

John hesitated. 'Suppose they take something?'

'Okay, go and ask the price and I will meet you back here.'

'All right,' he said reluctantly.

Anita walked quickly to the stable. Jerome and Babwe were just returning from behind the stable with the horses when they saw her coming towards them.

'Jerome, did you bring anything to eat… Babwe?'

Jerome looked at her for the first time since they left. All kinds of things raced through his mind. Alice, for one, kept haunting him whenever he confronted Anita. He did not know what to think.

'I only brought a roast potato,' said Jerome.

'That's what I have too,' said Babwe, not stopping to talk with Anita.

'Okay, I am getting some bread and milk; you all can

have some, if you want.'

'Sure, Miss Anita. We are starving,' Babwe shouted over his shoulder.

'Jerome, I miss you so much,' Anita said, as soon as Babwe was out of earshot. They stood facing each other.

'Where is John?' Jerome asked.

'He is back there checking out the price of the bread and butter. Can you meet me tonight at Hell House? I want you to hold me so much.'

'What time?'

'As soon as my father turns off the light.'

'About what time is that?'

'Near midnight. How will you know?'

'There is no moon tonight. I will have to guess.'

'Even if you don't see me, wait. If anyone is around, meet me at Lookout.'

'Okay.'

'Let us go back now.'

John had checked out the price of the bread and butter and returned to where Anita had been standing. He did not see her there so he decided to walk towards the stable. He looked ahead just in time to see Anita turning around with Jerome; Babwe was heading in his direction.

Oh! He wanted so much to be alone on this trip with Anita – those two slaves had spoiled his plans. He couldn't care less if they had starved to death. Anita was too soft-hearted and he would have to correct that. Nevertheless, he felt he was gaining more ground in his relationship with her. He laughed in triumph. John, you are doing great, he told himself. Anita didn't resist him at all during their shopping spree. It appeared as if she liked it when he placed his arms around her. He hadn't done that in a long time. She liked his jokes, too. The trip was worth it, he laughed silently. He wished it would never end.

Chapter Nine

Jerome had no way of knowing when it would be midnight. There was no moon, in fact the night was pitch black. He could only guess.

Jerome peered through the small hole of a window of his sleeping quarters. There wasn't much he could see, except the faint streak of yellow light coming from one of the windows of the master's house. The night was quiet, as quiet as the grave. The sounds of a few nocturnal insects broke the silence at times, but for the most part the stillness of the atmosphere was all that was around.

Sleep had left Jerome's eyes. When he came back from Junction it was about six o'clock. He quickly got something to eat, some stale bread and a bowl of cornmeal porridge, and off he went to bed. He must have been sleeping for about three hours when he suddenly sprang up as if someone was trying to strangle him. It was at that point he remembered his date and quickly ran over to the window. Babwe and the rest were fast asleep. The snores had died down and everyone was sleeping comfortably.

The young slave, who had been sleeping in his clothes, slipped out of the room, softly closing the door behind him but leaving a little opening for him to return.

He stepped out into the black night like a thief looking for his next victim. What a risk he was taking. That didn't enter his mind. The inviting figure of Anita gnawed at his mind and he wondered if he was in love as she seemed to be. Alice was not in his thoughts at that moment. All he could think about was the yearning and slender arms of Anita reaching out for him.

Jerome moved like a skilful prowler who knew where he was going and what his mission was all about. He looked east, west, north and south, to ensure he was not seen and that no one was coming. All was clear. He moved away from the old bunkhouse and headed towards the great white house, which stood sturdy and somewhat ghastly against the blackness of the night. Jerome was captured by nervousness as he passed it and moved in the direction of Hell House. Suppose John or Massa Alfred came bolting through those prison-like doors and grabbed him by the hand? It was not impossible, but a possibility, he thought. As he passed the house he looked back at it and became more nervous. Except for the main hall or living room area, the lights were all out.

Jerome walked stealthily to the huge star apple tree known as Hell House. He came to it, stopped, looked around and then felt for a protruding root he had sat on the last time he was there. It was there all right and he sat on it again. But this time it was under different circumstances. Jerome smiled broadly.

Something stirred over beside the well. Jerome, heart pounding thunderously pressed his body against the tree in fright. He could feel the rough bark scraping his back. There was someone out there. Before he could try to figure out what, or who it was, Jerome saw a figure loom large in front of him. It was a woman; it was Anita. Apparently, she had been sitting on the other side of the well and had seen him lurking under the tree.

She didn't say anything; asked no questions, nor sought to find out who the figure was under the tree. She came right up to him as if she knew exactly where he was sitting. Jerome saw her outline, despite the dark clothing she was wearing and came to his feet just in time to slip right into her waiting arms. Even at this point, she said nothing.

A combination of wet lips and tears crawled all over Jerome's face until the opening of his mouth was swallowed up by her tongue. She kissed him as hard as ever. It was the first time she had ever kissed a man so hard.

*

John lay sprawled in his rocking chair, looking out at the green cane fields before him. Very soon they would be ready. Very soon sharp machetes would sink into their juicy bodies and afterward they would be fed into the huge grinding trough and then ultimately to that large boiling pot. The latter was not his responsibility; his job was to ensure the canes were cut and removed from the field.

The upcoming crop would be big, from what he could see. He would earn some good money. John smiled, the smiling bursting out into a soft giggle. At the end of the crop marriage would be on his mind. What better time to think about it than on a Sunday morning when he didn't have to think about work. Furthermore, after a hard week's work and a nice little trip with Anita yesterday, now could be the time to thrive on the memories. One thing he was not certain about was whether he should propose marriage shortly after Lynda's arrival. He laughed aloud now. He told himself that if that was the only problem he had, then he had none. John smiled again; how silly one could get over a woman's love.

*

The rich, resonating voices echoed across the quiet valley. It had always been like that on a Sunday morning as slaves gathered to worship Massa God. They sang, danced, clapped and stomped their feet in jubilation. It was the only form of entertainment or opportunity to gather together and they did make use of that. Singing formed the bulk of the worship and a lot of slaves, both young and old, always looked forward to those Sunday morning meetings.

Alice Rowe was one of them. She never missed services. Nowadays, she had every reason not to, with the presence of Jerome on some Sundays. He had not been there the previous week and she was very anxious to see him this week.

Each time a song was finished Alice peered over her shoulder to see if Jerome had arrived. They were almost mid-way into the service when he arrived, taking his usual seat at the back. During the singing Alice slipped down to the back to join him.

'You are late,' she whispered, as she came to sit beside him.

'I slept late,' he said warily.

'You didn't go to bed early?'

'I was up late.'

'Doing what?'

'Thinking about you.'

She blushed and rejoined the singing.

After the service they rushed to their usual seat under a banana tree at the back of the church. Jerome held her hand as they talked.

'Y'know, I have been thinking about you a great deal of late.'

She smiled, her face illuminated by the compliment. 'Really, why?'

'Probably I have been missing you… too much.'

'Does that means you may want to see me more often?'

'I don't know. It's not possible right now.'

'So what can we do?'

'Make use of the time we have. It's only once a week and that is all we are going to get for now.'

'So I agree, we make the best use of it, but how?'

'We can probably slip away during church.'

'Are you crazy?' she said, getting a little serious.

'How?'

'Jerome. God is important to me. He is our only hope and I could never do that – no matter how much I love you, and I do, you understand?' She squeezed his hand.

Jerome bent over and kissed her softly. She returned it ravenously. The kiss confused him because right at that moment Anita's hungry kiss last night flooded his mind. He pulled away from Alice.

She looked at him in bewilderment.

'Are you all right Jerome? Is something wrong?'

'N-no, I-I thought or had a feeling someone was watching us,' he said, looking around.

She looked around and saw no one. 'Everybody is inside,' she said.

'Maybe it was just mind over matter.'

'You want to continue?' she said, looking away shyly.

'It's okay; we can pick up where we left off at another time.'

'I will certainly remind you about that.'

'Please do.'

'I will, for sure.'

'How are things over at your place?'

'They can't be anywhere worse.'

'The same here.'

'Many have hope that the abolitionist movement will gain momentum.'

'There has been talk over here too but I have not been getting much information.'

'I look forward to that day when we will be free people. Don't you?'

'Sure,' he said, Anita flashing across his mind again.

'Imagine if we are free Jerome. We won't need to hide

from anyone when we want to express our true feelings.'
She saw him looking into space. 'Are you with me Jerome?'

'O-oh, I am; in fact I was so taken up with that thought
that my mind strayed for a while.'

'Ha ha – it seems you are really anxious.'

*

Anita watched from her bedroom window as a few slaves
came trekking back from church. It was about five o'clock
and the only day they seemed to look forward to was almost
over.

Anita rarely visited church. She should probably go to
their church one day and see what it was like.

Alfred would undoubtedly be against that; nevertheless
it would be an experience she wouldn't want to miss. She
could see the look on their faces and it was all smiles.
Somehow, something, whatever that was, made them
happy and she was anxious to find out what.

Anita watched Jerome searchingly as he came up the
walkway with Maude. He seemed happy, too, talking
cheerfully with her. He looked a little extra handsome
today, maybe because of the better garb he was wearing.
Given adequate care that young man could become one
handsome chunk of flesh. She smiled, remembering their
encounter last night, and lamented on the cold reality of
being unable to see each other as often as she would have
liked.

She was almost certain she saw Jerome look up towards
her window. Jerome didn't know where her bedroom was
but she vowed he would know sometime in the future,
when their love had no need to remain a secret. That could
be painful for her parents. Nevertheless, what was important was her happiness. As far as she was concerned,
happiness to her was synonymous with Jerome.

Anita thought of John and laughed beneath her breath. She respected him for his sincerity and his company during her lonely times. But those days seemed to have passed now; she had entered a new phase of her life. Now, she was no longer lonely. She was the happiest girl in Jamaica.

Chapter Ten

A deathly silence fell over Jack's Place, slowly but surely. Another work week was looming. The threat of continuous labour, little rest, enough food to survive, and sweaty bodies rubbing against worn khaki clothes, hung in the minds of those who knew what it was like.

Sunday was a day to look forward to. Now, it was no more; as nightfall would rule for the next eleven hours. The next light of day would find them in the cane fields. There was little hope that the situation would change quickly. News of an uprising, or the efforts of the abolitionists, gave a little hope sometimes. However, when no news was forthcoming many lapsed back into hopelessness and depression.

Maude sat quietly in her old, creaky-looking chair, a stern expression on her face. She was worried. She had been summing up the events of the day as far as Jerome was concerned. She had seen him with Alice and they both seemed to have been enjoying each other's company. That was fine for Maude. But what about Anita? She had been walking on cloud nine all week. Anita had never been happier and Maude's sixth sense informed her that things were going well between her and Jerome. She didn't know how, but she had a funny suspicion that somehow, somewhere she was seeing him.

Maude knew sooner or later she would have to confront Jerome. As his 'mother', she would have a mother-to-son conversation with him. She feared the waters ahead for

Jerome could get muddy.

Maude fell asleep in her thoughts. Monday morning, she got up bright and early and fixed the men of the sleeping quarters their porridge, coffee and bread. In no time she headed for Massa's house to prepare breakfast for the family, and lunch and dinner later in the day, Anita was in her thoughts the whole morning. She committed herself to watching her every move from now on and to watching and noting what she said during their conversations.

*

Alice Rowe felt like a queen today. Her conversation with Jerome yesterday made her feel like a more mature woman. She, too, was on top of the world. Jerome's words echoed back into her ears each time his smiling face flashed across her mind.

Was she that lucky to be able to fall in love with an articulate, intelligent, handsome, and considerate young man like him? Was she in dreamland, or it was real?

Alice pinched herself to be convinced she was not dreaming. She had to stop doing the laundry in order to do that. A pair of cold but admiring eyes bulged out at her from beneath the broad straw hat. They had been watching her swaying hips reacting to the movement of her hands as she scrubbed away at the dirt-soaked clothes of her master. It was the very master himself watching his clothes being washed. He was not interested in the cleaning of the clothes. He was lusting after the body that was in front of him. Larry Daniels had been doing that ever since Alice entered her teenage years, five years ago.

He had watched her develop into a slender and attractive young woman. On the other hand, Mr Daniels was a swarthy-looking middle-aged man, who looked like he lacked iron and all the essential vitamins. He looked pale all the time, cranky, and walked like he was going to fall on his chin. Yet his appetite for sexual satisfaction, especially from young wenches, had never waned. Larry concluded it was now time to start making a move – on Alice.

'Are you tired my dear?' he asked softly.

Alice, very much startled at the voice from behind, spun around to face her grinning master. 'Uh... uh Massa I... I am okay,' she mumbled, her voice breaking in fright.

'Don't be nervous, I won't bite. I am only here to let you know how much I appreciate the way you have been doing the laundry,' said the plantation owner.

'Thanks Massa Daniels, thanks a lot sir.'

'It's okay, you don't have to say sir.'

She was a little puzzled. 'Yes sir.'

Larry laughed, exposing perfect teeth. 'I will be seeing you soon,' he smiled and walked away towards his house.

That was a strange visit, Alice thought. Strange indeed. She stared after him in disbelief. Larry was a wealthy man. His plantation was much larger than Jack's; he had more slaves and a very lucrative tobacco plantation, one of the few in the region. He had no children, only a brother who lived in England. His banker, bookkeeper and lawyer were his only close friends. He entertained them quite regularly.

Alice never thought for one moment that Larry wanted something from her. Her first impression was that he had no interest in women at all. She returned to her laundry, and almost immediately her thoughts jumped back to Jerome.

★

'Howdy,' said Jerome, as he stepped into the kitchen after another weary day's work.

'Hi son. How was the day?' Maude was glad to hear from him. After all, she had become so anxious to have a talk with him.

'Can't be worse.'

Maude came closer to him and patted Jerome on the shoulder. 'Don't you worry son. It cannot be like this all the time.'

Jerome sat down on an old wooden bench near a coal stove. He scratched his head like a wizard. 'You know, Aunt Maude, I often wonder about that.'

'What do you mean?'

'Whether slavery will ever end.'

'What are you talking about?' she whispered. 'You have not been hearing the reports?'

'Reports of what?'

'The abol… what they call them?'

'Abolitionists.'

'Yes. That's right, the abol… the abolitionists from England have been coming to Spanish Town regularly to talk with the Governor about ending slavery.'

'That's just talk…'

'I don't think so. Slaves are holding secret meetings too.'

'Where?' he said, looking around as if the meetings were taking place nearby.

'I don't know. It's being kept very secret. Only a few people know.'

'They are having them in Big Yard too?'

'Maybe, maybe not. I don't know.'

'Well, that sounds a little encouraging.'

'My son. Let us continue to pray to Massa God that we will live to see the end of this vicious system. We have a lot to gain.'

'Yes – our freedom,' he said, clenching his fist. 'If I could only know where those meetings are being held.'

'You would go?'

'Of course,' he said, nodding his head.

'You have thought about that long and hard.'

'Yes, Aunty.'

'You know the consequences?'

'Consequences?'

'Yes. You could be hanged if caught.'

'What?'

'Hanged by the neck. Plantation owners wouldn't even wait on the law. Why do you think Massa Alfred has been having all those night meetings?'

'Why?'

'They want to make sure the abolitionists don't come here to entice the slaves.'

Jerome rubbed his jaw, a little troubled. 'Does Miss Anita know about the meetings?'

Maude paused. 'You should know,' she said, looking away from his stare.

'M-me? But how?'

'I know my son. I know.'

'Know what, Auntie?'

Maude said beside him. 'I know Jerome.' She patted his back. 'You don't have to worry about your little secret. It may not be a secret any longer but it is safe with me.'

Jerome was stunned. 'How did you know?' he mumbled.

'My son, I am old enough to know when a woman is interested in a man. And as far as I can see, she is head over heels after you. She loves you to death.'

'What should I do?'

'I know you must be confused. I have pondered over it at nights, because there is Alice…'

'Alice… yes Alice, a lovely girl I don't want to lose.'

'It could be very dangerous, Anita's love for you, if it is ever exposed. I know that is why it is safe with me. I suspect Babwe senses something too but it is also safe with him.'

'I know.'

'Anita's love is a love for tomorrow, my son. It may never be able to flourish because of our circumstances.'

'We have to be free, and even then we would not be really free in a sense, because she is white.'

'Exactly.'

'I have thought long and hard about that.'

'On the other hand, my son, if she loves you, and I know she does, with her wealth, you could get a good start after we are free.'

'Hmmm; I was not looking at it from that angle, you know.'

'We have to look at it from all angles. Our day is coming soon. I can feel it in my veins. We have to grab what we can now so long as we know what we are doing.'

'What should I do, then?'

Maude thought for a while before she answered. 'Son, I want the best for you.'

'I know, Aunty.'

'Your parents left you in my care. I knew them from childhood. I have no children. You are my only responsibility and I want the best for you.'

'I know, Aunty,' he said again, tears swelling up in his eyes.

'I will go to the end to make sure you get the best because you deserve it. Alice is a nice girl.'

'That's true.'

'Anita is a beautiful woman, too.'

'I agree.'

'The two want your love. However, a day will come when you will have to chose.'

'I know.'

'You want to live with someone or marry someone for the rest of your life who you will be happy with.'

'Yes Aunty.'

She patted his back again. 'While I would want you to

have Alice as your wife, at the same time, you must think about what is it that Anita can offer you without hurting her, or hurting yourself. It may be that you will have to love her but can't live with her. Your job Jerome may be to get that thought across to her.'

'She is crazy over me. I don't know how I could ever do that right now.'

'I don't mean right now, but as time goes by you make your plan and carry it out at the right moment.'

'That sounds reasonable. But what about Alice?'

'Let me handle her. Try not to see her every Sunday. I will fill in for you until things become a little clearer. You have to be very careful about John, let me warn you. He is madly in love with Anita and even one slight hint that Anita wants you and my son, you are a goner.'

'You don't have to tell me – I know.'

'How often do you meet Anita?'

'How do you know I meet her?'

'Listen Jerome. I work with her every day and I have seen the change since we went to Malvern. She can't say it but I know she is in love, but not with John for sure.'

'Well I see her maybe every two weeks at Hell House.'

'Be careful. Be careful. Go behind the well. It is much safer there.'

'I think so too. Have you said anything to Alice about her?'

'Of course not! How could I ever do that?'

'Thanks Aunty. We are in this together from now on and I need your help badly, probably Babwe's too.'

'I believe he already knows and we might as well bring him in on this. I will talk to him.'

'No need to. He knew long before you.'

'God is on our side as long as we don't do anything foolish. Slavery will soon be no more and that will be our time to make our move,' she said confidently.

'It seems as if you had this all planned out.'

'Not really. I ponder about it sometimes but I wanted to be absolutely certain about the relationship. Now that I am, we must plan for your future.'

'Thanks again, Aunty. I want to get something to eat and then off to bed to face another wretched day,' he said, planting a kiss on her cheek.

'Don't worry, time is the master.'

Chapter Eleven

Another week dragged on wearily, and the tired souls of those who worked the sugar plantations yearned for some kind of relief. The harvest was winding down, but as one crop was over, another one began.

Plantation owner Campbell was all smiles. It had been a bountiful harvest for sugar. The price being fetched in England was far better than expected. It came at just the right time because Lynda would be here just in time to hear the good news. She was arriving in three days, if the weather permitted.

Tomorrow morning, Thursday, he along with Anita, Maude, Babwe and Jerome, would journey into the Jamaican capital – Spanish Town – to meet Lynda. John would have to take care of the plantation until they returned. He acted as though he would have wanted to go, but he knew that it was useless to argue because there was no one else really to oversee the operations. He was hoping that Anita would remain behind but the chances of that were ninety nine to one. Again, he felt defeated; he was angry.

Maude, Jerome and Babwe were more than happy for the trip. They knew Anita was behind the choice; and why. Slowly, but surely, it could be the beginnings of greater things to come as long as she had eyes for Jerome.

The journey would take nearly three days, if they could utilise the daylight hours as much as possible. It would be a hard journey but it was more than welcome for them all, especially Anita.

She smiled in triumph. Her father didn't argue about the travel crew. And once again, Anita had won round two.

The journey would probably provide little opportunity for Anita and Jerome to have time together. Nevertheless, all she wanted was to have him in her presence. She would capitalise on any opportunity to be with him; she would have four eyes from the moment the journey began. But before the trip – before her mother came – she had to have one rewarding last fling.

Alfred had retired to bed early. He had advised Anita to do likewise. That she promised to do, but only after she put her plan into action.

As soon as the lights were out she would wait for that moment she had been waiting for. Anita had her tea and was sitting around the mahogany dining table when she heard a rap on the door.

'Who could that be?' she whispered. Surely not the person she was expecting. She went up to the door. 'Who's there?'

'Me. John.'

'Oh…' She grimaced. John was the last person she wanted to see. 'What brings you here? I was just about to go to bed,' she said, opening the door.

'S-sorry m'love, I-I just wanted to say… to be with you before you leave in the morning.'

'That won't be necessary, John. I am okay and furthermore, I need to get some rest.'

John was hoping she would invite him in but she still held the door half open. 'I am really sorry but a few minutes won't do much harm.'

Anita tried very hard to contain her anger. 'Dad was insistent that I get some sleep so I promised him I would.'

'Oh, is he asleep?'

'He went to bed about ten minutes ago.'

'I see. I won't bother then, I will see you in the morning.'

'See you then. Have a good night, John.'

He hesitated a bit. But that goodnight kiss he had been expecting was nowhere in sight. He realised that and so walked away.

He walked down the steps, flinging his feet carelessly against the cut stones. The thought of that lonely bed haunted him. Anita seemed tired, he admitted, and being the kind of gentleman he thought he was, it was best that he left her alone. There was not another eligible bachelor for many miles around, so the thought of Anita having someone else was a long shot. However, he must not give up his fight for her. He would win her eventually; he just had to be patient.

John was moving towards the side of the house, in the direction of the foremen's quarters and office, when he thought he saw something move across the lawn in front of him. The only thing blocking his view from that vantage point was a small clump of croton trees. He stopped in his tracks. John's eyes made a one hundred and eighty degree turn, surveying everything he could focus on in the dark. Nothing – nothing unusual. Should he take a closer look at the crotons? Nothing could be hiding there that he could not see. If curiosity killed the cat then he could be killed tonight; he wanted to take a look. Suppose whatever movement he saw had something to do with the abolitionist movement? Suppose arson was in the making, as had been the case in at least two plantations in the east? He had a duty to investigate.

John's knees wobbled with the thought of an uprising. He dismissed the thought and stepped towards the crotons. They were about four feet tall. It would not be difficult to see if anything was there. He wished he had taken his pistol with him; his only weapon would be his huge fists and his thick leather boots.

John was within a yard of the trees. He stopped, looked around and then back at the crotons. He made a circle, watching for any movement that was out of the norm. Again, nothing. He came yet a little closer. He thought he saw something but before he could figure out anything he felt a cold object make contact with the back of his head. Then he saw some stars; not the ones above but stars which sank him into a world of blackness he had never seen before.

★

Jerome was the first to get out of his slumber. It was a restless night for him. He could not sleep, mainly because of two things that were on his mind. He was nervous but relieved that he had given John something to think about – if he was alive and secondly, he knew Anita would be disappointed that he hadn't lived up to his end of the bargain – their date, under last night's circumstances she would understand.

When he slammed John in the head with the dried root of an old croton tree, he didn't stop to see if he had got up from the fall. He was so frightened that he ran as fast as a cheetah to his bed. Certainly, John could not have known it was him because he attacked from behind. John had started to circle the crotons and all Jerome did was move in the opposite direction in a wider angle and then crept up towards him and charged.

Jerome had heard the heavy thud of his boots as soon as he made the corner of the house. He had nowhere to hide but in the crotons. He stood behind them, watching John's every move. The advantage he had was that while he could see John, John could not see him. It was easy to tell it was John because of his burly figure and loud shoe. Many slaves knew that trademark, too, because he often kicked them with it, leaving a mark.

Anita and her father were out early, too. Everyone was ready and waiting in the twilight of what would be another hot and sticky day.

Jerome watched Anita cautiously. He had hoped to take a quick look at the place where he had hit John to see if he was there but time did not allow for that. Anita's face was expressionless and he tried to meet her gaze. There was none.

'Are we all ready here?' asked Alfred.

'Yes, suh,' said Jerome.

'You are ready for this journey, young man?'

'Yes, suh, I am ready.'

'Good.'

John emerged from the shadows – a great relief for Jerome.

'You look as if a mule kicked you last night,' said Alfred.

'I just had a rough night. That's all.'

'Are you sure you will be okay here?'

'Sure sir. I will take care.'

Anita looked at him. He really looked miserably restless. 'Tonight, you try to get some sleep, okay?'

John was glad to hear that. 'I will honey, you have a good journey and do take care.' Those kind words from Anita seemed to make his day.

'If everything goes as planned we should be back around Tuesday night,' said Alfred. 'John,' he said, patting him on the shoulder, 'I have confidence in you; just keep your eyes open for any trouble,' he whispered, not wanting Anita to hear the latter part of the statement.

'Bye, sir and you have a good trip. I hope Lynda will be here on time.'

'I hope so too.'

'Bye John. I will be seeing you,' Anita bent and gave him

a kiss on the cheek. That one would make his week.

Jerome saw it but pretended that he didn't. He felt jealous but what could he have done?

They all took their respective positions on the buggy. Their supplies were neatly packed, the horses were raring to go, and they all did just that.

John watched the buggy speed away into the coming light of day. It wouldn't be that bad after all. Anita had him on her mind, he concluded. She was really nice to him.

John didn't want to upset Alfred's journey so he refrained from telling him about last night's encounter with the unknown. He had been lying there for about ten minutes when he realised what had happened. The aftermath left him puzzled. Who could that have been? A runaway slave from this plantation or some other? Today, he would have to take a roll call.

*

Three hours away from Yardley Chase and the team was going great guns. They had probably covered about fifteen miles, which was great going. Not much was said and the only noise seemed to be that of the sound of hooves on the dirt road. Anita hadn't seen Jerome all morning. She pretended that he did not exist. On the contrary, Jerome tried on several occasions to meet her glance.

She did look back on a couple of occasions on what had been going on up front where Babwe and Jerome were leading the team. Whether it was just a sham or not Jerome didn't know. How long would she avoid him?

All along the journey, Jerome felt relieved that nothing had happened to John. John hadn't given any indication that he was a suspect. That was good. With him in the clear so far, the journey could turn out as another good one. But would it? How could it when the woman who claimed to be madly in love with him was giving him the cold shoulder? He knew the depth of her disappointment over his non-appearance; to feel his powerful arms and body swallow her in a world of unspeakable pleasure. But what else could he have done? Jerome felt he deserved a chance to explain. Would he get that chance under the present circumstances?

Chapter Twelve

Larry Daniels had waited impatiently for this day. It was long overdue, but it had to come sooner or later. Everyone was hard at work in the field, even his wife. As a man who was supposed to be sick, Larry should be in bed. Indeed, he was in bed, only it was for a different reason.

Larry listened from under his thick blanket for the creak from the door, to signal its opening. Alice would come in to make the bed, and he could visualise her young body swaying to and fro as she tidied up the room. Larry had told Sarah he wasn't feeling well and that she should see that everything went okay in the field. She wanted to do that, not even being that concerned about Larry's health.

Larry smiled; a sneaky smile that had a touch of something sinister. He would have little opposition because all the other slave women, most of them middle-aged like he was, would be down in the kitchen, Alice was the only one who looked after his room.

He heard the sound that he wanted to hear. His eyes quickly focused on the object in the doorway; it moved in his direction and came to a halt right before his bed. Alice stopped and took a second look at what was turning out to be the shape of someone under the covers. She came closer. She wanted to touch it but was uncertain if she should. At that moment, she came within reach of the hands which had been waiting to grab her. The hands reached out and clasped around hers like a handcuff. She was frightened.

'Huh… Wh-who is it?'

'It is me, my love. I am here, for you,' said Larry with a grin. Before she could say another word both hands reached out and pulled her down on the bed. It all happened so quickly she didn't have time to respond – to resist or to assist. The next thing she knew she was lying on top of a naked man and his hands were far up under her dress. In fact, too far.

★

'Hey boys, out here is good country. We should probably get some steers grazing out there,' grinned Alfred.

'Sure, Massa. The grass look really good,' responded Babwe in a toothless grin.

'It seems like nothing is happening out here. All that land going to waste.'

'Would you seriously buy it, Dad?' asked Anita, as she joined the dialogue.

'Not really, but it looks tempting.'

'Buy it if you can afford it.'

'What? Are you serious?'

'I am.'

'Who will manage it?'

'I would.'

'What? You would?'

'Of course. You don't think I could manage?'

'Well,' he said, his hands fumbling under his chin. 'Maybe that is something to think about.'

Babwe wanted to say something but wasn't certain what he should say.

'All I would need is some good and strong hands to help me.'

'What about security?'

Anita knew that a possible uprising was on her father's mind. 'That is why I need the strong hands.'

'Let me think about it.'

'Good. I will keep reminding you about your promise, Dad.'

'You do that, my dear.'

Jerome was a quiet listener all along, Anita would never give up in her attempt to find a suitable environment for their relationship to flourish in. A plantation out here with him on it would be a perfect opportunity for her.

The party had just passed the parish border and was now ascending the Spur Tree Hills. From that point, some one thousand feet up, they could look down on the vast valley below, which stretched all the way out to the beginning of the Santa Cruz Mountain range. By nightfall they would have covered about ten miles and would bed down in a town called Porus, which was perched on the border with the adjoining parish – Clarendon. The next parish to that was St Catherine, where the capital was located, the biggest parish on the island.

Lunchtime brought them to a halt under a huge oak tree on the journey up Spur Tree Hills. There was no river anywhere near this area of the island Christopher Columbus had described as 'land of wood and water', and 'the fairest eyes have ever beheld'.

'Get the horses some fresh grass,' Alfred told Jerome as soon as the buggy came to a halt.

'Yes, suh.'

Maude and Babwe were the first to leave the buggy. Maude took the food down and after little hesitation found an appropriate spot under the tree. Anita's eyes never left Jerome, combing the enticing body that she knew was under those weather-beaten clothes. He seemed not too concerned about her now; but she was not worried, given the circumstances. She had her plans on what would take place on the trip.

Maude had the food ready within minutes and everyone

devoured their share like half-starved hyenas. Jerome was the only one left to have his own, and Anita had a small amount of bread remaining. Alfred got up from his seating position and so did Babwe and Maude.

Jerome had finished with the horses and was coming for his lunch when he met Alfred on the way.

'Are they still eating?' he asked.

'Yes, suh. They haven't been wasting any time.'

'Good. Get something to eat and we will be on our way.'

'Yes, suh.'

Jerome strode towards the spot where he saw a blanket that they had been sitting on. Maude was packing up, Babwe was sitting by the buggy and Anita was still sitting, nibbling at something.

'Here is yours,' said Maude, handing him the food and then walking away towards the buggy.

'Thanks, Aunty.' He was about to walk away too.

'You can sit,' said Anita.

Jerome looked in the direction of her father, indicating that he could be watching them.

'It is okay. We were all sitting together here.'

'Let's be careful.'

'What happened last night?' She could not wait any longer to hear the reason. For most of the journey, that had been foremost on her mind.

'It is a long story,' he said. He seemed more interested in the food than anything else.

'Something happened?'

'Yes.'

'What?'

'I can't tell you now.'

'All right. Tonight I will try to see you while everyone is asleep. Be on the look out.'

'Is that possible?'

'I think it is. I will make it possible. I am longing for

you, Jerome. My skin is burning, my heart is aching and my mind is engulfed in thoughts beyond my comprehension.'

'I miss you too,' he said.

'Good. That means we want to see each other tonight. I am going to join my father.' She reached out and put her hands over his.

★

'Do you see what I see?' said Maude to Babwe.

'I saw before you – in fact I knew long before you.'

'He told me everything.'

'I can only wish things work out right.'

'Me too. We could all be free soon.'

'Wishful thinking. Yet it could happen.'

'Hmm. Let us hope for the best. The trouble is Anita is not even afraid anyone will find out.'

'I know… not even her father.'

'Right. We have to be on guard for both of them.'

'That is why she wanted us to come with her.'

'I realise that and to be honest with you I don't mind it at all.'

'Who would.'

Anita looked at her father admiringly.

'In two days you will see her, Dad.'

Alfred paused, looked at her and then smiled. 'I can hardly wait. I guess you can't either.'

'Yes, I miss her.'

He came up to her and hugged her like a long lost child. 'She must be missing us too. We are all lonely people,' he laughed.

'We are and we can only hope that will change soon,' she said.

He withdrew from the hold. 'How's John these days? Have you been seeing each other a lot?' he asked, out of the blue.

'Well. John has been coming around a lot these days and I don't know.'

'You are not sure about him?'

'Right. I don't know if he is the right person for me.'

'John is a nice guy who works very hard.'

'I know, Dad. He is a nice man, nice company, but I am still not certain.'

'I think John would make you a good husband. In a situation like this you need a good husband – you are getting on in age.'

'That is true.'

'I believe John will provide for you all that you need.'

'I have no doubt about that.'

'Then why you are so uncertain?'

'It is about things that you probably won't understand.'

'I guess so, but I am still recommending that you give it a try or continue to give it a try, nevertheless.'

'I don't even know if I want to do that.'

'Why not?'

Anita bowed her head, not wanting to look at her father. 'I don't want to let him feel everything is fine when it is not.'

'That is true, but at least you can establish an understanding.'

'John is the type of person who can get swell-headed and I really don't know how to deal with that.'

'Well my dear,' he said, putting both hands on her shoulders, 'you will have to decide what to do.'

'Thanks, Father.'

'By the way, do you see any other young man around the area that could, you know…' he teased.

Anita smiled broadly. 'As soon as I see one Dad, you will be the first to know.'

'Good girl.'

'And promise me one thing, Dad.'

'What?'

'That you will approve of him.'

'Your choice is my choice,' he laughed. 'I trust you on that.'

'Good.'

They resumed the uphill journey. The afternoon sun was merciless on them. They basked in its intense heat, hoping to reach Porus before nightfall. Whenever they passed under huge oak and cedar trees they welcomed the shade and relief they provided from the hot afternoon sun.

There wasn't much talk on the journey. Anita slept most of the time, while her father's eyes never left the road. She expected that of him; he didn't say it but he was wary of runaway slaves attacking or robbing them for food, or looting and shooting in anticipation of a slave rebellion. There had been talk of a few incidents of that nature and, of course, plantation owners would be the first to exercise caution.

Alfred reflected on the conversation he had had with his daughter. He was convinced that John would be the ideal husband for her. He was knowledgeable on the operations of the plantation. Everything in his will would go to Anita and she would need a strong man at her side whenever she took over.

She needed to be encouraged. With Lynda's presence, that task would probably be easier. As far as he could see Yardley Chase was very short of young men. He wished more of them would leave England for the tropical climate.

Porus was a sleeping town. Not much was happening when the buggy rolled down its main thoroughfare. It was getting dark and that was maybe the reason. The huge hotel sign could not be overlooked because it was one of the first buildings to be seen. A few buggies already occupied the space in front of it, so they had to park along the side of the building. Most of the people around were white folks; the only black person they saw was a slave driving a woman on her buggy on the way out of town.

Babwe and Jerome emptied the buggy of the needed gear and took it to the back of the building. Maude accompanied them, looking tired and exhausted from the journey. A few minutes later, Alfred came to tell them that they would have to bunk it under the buggy, Maude included. She had done that on several occasions so it was nothing new to her. Normally she would have stayed with Anita, however, the hotel only had one room available.

Anita wasn't certain whether it was a good thing or not. If Maude was with her it would have been ideal; she could easily sneak out. But with her father around, her protective father, she could take no chance at all. She would have to wait and see.

Chapter Thirteen

It was a tough day, John Stewart had to admit. It was probably one of the toughest in a long time. The slaves were somewhat lethargic no amount of yelling or screaming could have persuaded them to move those machetes faster. Or, perhaps there was another reason. Could it have been a silent protest in light of considerable progress in the abolition movement? A week ago, a huge plantation in southern St James, an adjoining parish, was gutted by fire. Arson was suspected and runaway slaves were said to be the culprits.

His attacker last night. The recollection stunned his confused mind. Did it have anything to do with the movement? Or could it have been done by a slave he had punished and was only trying to get back at him? The more he thought of the possibilities, the more he became confused.

John turned his thoughts to Anita. His lone presence in his bunk reminded him of what life could be with her in it. He smiled. But the smile quickly turned to a stern look when he thought of her strange behaviour at times. Many nights he had tossed and turned on his bed, thinking and wondering if there was anyone else in her life. He could not come up with anyone. There were too few men around the area and those that he could think of were already involved with someone else. What then? Why had there been a change in her attitude? Sometimes he did not want to believe that she had changed. He even told himself that it was his imagination. Yet there were times he was convinced that she had changed.

For one, she had refused on two occasions to go to a dance with him. She had gone to Junction with him, however, she did so reluctantly, and furthermore she wanted to be accompanied by slaves. What was up her sleeve?

John sat up in his bed as a thought came to his mind. He glanced up at the window at the dark sky outside, imagining Anita in her lonely bed at some inn or hotel, just wanting someone – even him – to come and lay down beside her. If that someone who would be with her was not John Stewart then he must find out who it was. He thumped his chest in anticipation of his success with this new plan. John: you are a smart ass, he told himself. Very soon he would know who, if anyone, was involved in Anita's precious life.

★

A creeping silence came over the town of Porus. The town had fallen into deep sleep. Not even a stray dog was in sight. Main Street was empty and, except for a few lamp-posts, only a light shone from the hotel's batwing doors.

The whole town might have been asleep, but not Anita, although she was the first to jump into bed. Alfred was easily taken in by her act, and shortly after he spread a blanket on the floor and went into another world as fast as he had laid down the blanket.

Anita wanted to be certain that he was asleep, so she waited for those snores that were his trademark. They came one hour later; and to be certain that his sleep was deep and would last for the next eight hours she gave him one more hour. After it came, in her estimation, she made her move.

Anita was skilful in many things. Of late, she had gained considerable skill in opening doors without making a sound. This she did with her bedroom door, which led right to where the buggy was parked. Anita tiptoed out to where the buggy was, looking ahead in the dark to see who was who. What a chance she was taking. Maude would be under the buggy; Babwe possibly on top and probably Jerome to the side. She only had to look at the sizes on top of the buggy or to the side of it. She would not bother to look under it because it was a foregone conclusion that Maude would be there.

One step at a time was how Anita made her move. She did not have much time but she wanted to ensure she did not do anything wrong. She approached the dark clump that was supposed to be Jerome. She got nervous, tense and even anxious. The figure was that of a man all right, and right away she had no doubts whose it was. Her face lit up in the dark and her feet shuffled a little faster. Without even thinking about what she was about to do, Anita parted the blanket and slid under it.

★

'I can hardly wait to see Mom,' Anita giggled.

'You seem to be in a good mood today,' her father grinned.

'I am.'

'Did you have a good night's sleep?'

'I slept like a baby in the arms of her father,' she said.

Alfred looked around at her, 'I thought you would have said Mom.'

'That's because she is not here yet,' she teased.

'Oh, aren't you smart!'

'I am your daughter, remember.'

'I remember – you could outsmart any wise old dad.'

'I wonder why you say that,' she mused.

'Nothing. I…'

Anita suddenly became nervous. 'You think I am that smart?'

'Sure you are. I can't help but admire how mature you have got ever since you came to this island.'

'Really?'

'Yes and I think your mom will be proud of you.'

'Let us hope she is.'

'I think she will.'

'Let's hope she will like it here, too.'

'I have no doubts about that. She always wanted to live in the tropics.'

'Sometimes I forget what she looks like.'

'Are you serious?'

'I am.'

'Don't worry, you will soon see her again.'

'And this time it will be for a long time.'

'Sure it will be – probably until you get married.'

Anita turned to meet his glance. 'Married? I was not even thinking about that, Dad.'

'Well, any concerned father would have that on his mind almost all the time.'

'I don't blame you for that, Dad. In fact, I admire you for it. It's only that I wasn't even thinking about that.'

'It is okay, I understand.'

'I know how you feel about John, but Dad, with due respect, I am beginning to see more and more every day that I really don't have any feelings for him.'

Alfred's face became serious and even more concerned. 'If you need time to decide then so be it.'

'I am not even sure time will make a difference.'

'There is no one else around?'

'Someone will come in time, Dad, don't you worry.'

'You seem so certain, my dear.'

'I am.'

'Is there something you are not telling me?'

'Not necessarily.'

'What do you mean?

'One day, one day you will see.'

'A surprise?'

'You could say that.'

'Ha ha ha, I tell you that you are smart. I mean it. You are one heck of a gal.' Alfred laughed so loud that Jerome had to look around at him.

★

Alice felt ashamed. How could such a thing ever happen or be allowed to happen to her? Worst of all, she had no one to talk to about it. Sarah was out and so were the other women she knew, most of whom could not keep their mouths shut. Maude was the only person she could relate to; however, she only saw Maude on Sundays, It would have to wait until the next one, or the following one, as she had hinted that she might be going to Spanish Town to meet Mrs Campbell.

Larry was a snake; a worthless old and cruel man she thought was like a father to her. She despised him now; she couldn't bear to look at him. He wanted a sex slave and she was the target. If Sarah ever knew, all hell would break loose. Sarah was like a mother and how could she ever tell her what her 'father figure' had done to her without hurting her? It had to remain a secret, not because she wanted it to but because of the possible consequences.

Jerome! She felt guilty. Alice felt at fault and as if she had cheated on the only love she had ever had. How would she ever hide that guilt? She had not eaten anything all day. Her appetite had left her.

★

Two days later, Alfred and his troops rolled into the Jamaican capital. It was a long and hard journey and the sight of the city was a welcome relief. Spanish Town was huge and never before had any of the slaves seen such a sprawling city, with all the modern luxuries one could think of. It was buggy town: slaves were all around, young girls and boys, buyers and sellers of all kinds of merchandise, including slaves. The buildings were many and varied. Spanish Town not only had a main street but many others running horizontally and vertically to it.

It was midday. Alfred headed straight to the shipping agent's office to get more details about the arrival of the boat from England. The port was about a mile away from the town centre.

'The boat came in about half an hour ago,' a burly-looking agent told Alfred.

'Here already?' he yelled in fright.

'Yes sir. Good weather all the way, I am told sir.'

'Come on, let's go,' Alfred came running to the others, almost too happy to communicate the information to them.

'When is the boat coming?' Anita asked.

'It is already here, honey.'

'What?'

'It came half an hour ago,' Alfred said storming up to the buggy. She must be waiting and wondering if something has happened.

Anita felt very happy and relieved.

She looked at Jerome. Their glances met and both of them smiled.

The journey to the wharf took about half an hour. As they approached the rusty old wharf, Alfred could see a number of women assembled beneath the dilapidated arrival station. His eyes searched diligently for that familiar face. It wasn't there. He came nearer and he looked a little bit closer but could see no one.

Anita had been looking too, but without success.

The buggy came to a halt and Anita and Alfred alighted, leaving the rest behind.

'I can hardly wait to see the mistress,' said Maude, yawning.

'Hmmmm, Miss Anita and Massa feel the same way too. How about your mother-in-law,' teased Babwe, looking at Jerome.

'Be careful Babwe. Don't ever say that again.'

'He is right,' interjected Maude. 'You cannot be too careful.'

'Okay, I guess you are right.'

'I don't know if her coming is either good or bad,' said Jerome, staring at a poster on the wall before him. He pointed at it and all three tried to figure out what was written on it. Maude could read very little, Babwe not at all. From what Jerome could glean, it was advertising an upcoming meeting being held by a group or organisation that was working to abolish slavery.

Jerome was encouraged by what he saw. He remembered pointing out to Babwe an old, burnt-out plantation he had seen at the Clarendon–St Catherine border. Was the uprising the reason? Probably, he would never know.

Jerome's thoughts were interrupted by the giggling, hugging and kissing that came towards the buggy. He turned to look into the eyes of one of the most beautiful woman he had ever seen. She was beautiful because she reminded him of someone else. Lynda Campbell was the split image of her daughter, or was it the other way around? Anita was the dead stamp of her mother. Jerome was not even certain; the only thing he was sure about was the reality of her beauty. What effect, if any, would this beauty have on their clandestine activities?

Chapter Fourteen

It had been one happy family at Jack's Place over the past two weeks. With Lynda's arrival, Anita and Alfred were busy people. The house was a buzz of activities, from tea parties to dinner parties. John tried hard not to be left out of anything. In fact, it seemed he was more often at the house than at work.

John found Lynda to be a pleasant person. That, he considered a plus for his plans. He tried several times to get her attention but to no avail. However, his luck changed today, a cold, dark and grey Sunday afternoon.

John was strolling across the lawn when he saw Lynda pruning some flowers.

'They are happy to see you,' he grinned.

'Hi, John. I guess you could say that.'

'If they could speak, they would surely be saying that.'

'Maybe someday they will.'

'It seems like you have been fitting in somehow.'

'As a matter of fact, I think I am.'

'Glad to know that, because out here in the tropics, some people take a lot of time to adjust to the new environment.'

'I have been longing to come here so much that I could fit into anything.'

'I see what you mean.'

'Anita… I missed her so much; she is growing into one heck of a woman. I am so glad I am here to see her and to give her whatever guidance I can.'

'Anita is truly a fine young woman.'

'Are there many young men around?' she said from out of the blue.

'Why? Oh, I see what you mean. Well, to be honest with you, there aren't any around – and even I myself wish there were a few. At least then I would have a few friends.'

'You don't?'

'Not really,' he said, scratching his head. 'W-well I should probably let you know that Anita—'

'You are seeing each other?'

John's face sparkled with delight. 'She told you that?'

'No.'

His face sank a little in disappointment. 'Then who?'

'Alfred and I were discussing her future when your name came up. Alfred seems to like you.'

Once again, a pleasant look came over his fleshy, sun-burnt face.

'Frankly, I think you are a nice fellow too.'

'Thanks, ma'am. That really means a lot to me.'

'John, how does Anita feel about you? Alfred seems to believe she has not made up her mind.'

'What? Are you certain about that?'

'He seems… I probably shouldn't be telling you this.'

'Go on Mrs Campbell, there is nothing to fear.'

'Well, Alfred is wondering if she may be seeing someone else. Do you know anything about that?'

John jerked his head, shock ripples tickling throughout his nervous system. 'I… I have to admit I have been wondering myself.'

Lynda turned her attention from the flowers to John. Concern was obvious by the look on her face. 'Do you have any reason to believe that?'

'Huh? None at all. In fact, I have even been doing my own investigations and so far I am unable to come up with anything.'

'So there may not be any truth to Alfred's assumption at all?'

'I can assure you that if she was seeing anyone else I would know. If there is someone that I don't know of, then I will find out,' said John remembering his plan.

'We are with you on this John. We want to see our daughter making the right decision and we will do anything regarding that.'

'I appreciate your trust in me and I have every intention of honouring my promise. Good day ma'am.'

'Good luck, John, and keep me informed.'

'Sure will ma'am.'

Lynda had finished her gardening and was walking past Hell House. Anita was sitting by the well, the afternoon breeze waving her hair.

'You look so lovely sitting there,' said Lynda, 'but you look sad too. Is everything okay?'

'Oh Mom! I am fine. I am here recalling the good times I've had right at this very spot.'

'Really? How?'

'Reading, looking around and admiring the beauty of the place and even talking to Maude.'

'Maude?'

'Yes Mom, Maude. She has been like a mother to me.'

'Well, well is that so? Has she been that good?'

'Yes Mom.'

'A slave woman?'

'Yes Mom – a slave woman.'

Lynda's expression changed. 'I may not be needed any-more then.'

'C'mon Mom, what are you talking about? You are my mother. Nothing can change that.'

'I know that but there are times when a mother's ab-sence can create a vacuum that needs to be filled. And you know what? It can be filled by anyone, even a slave woman.'

'Mom, are you jealous?' Anita asked, looking around at her.

'Jealous? No! Concerned? Yes.'

'About what?'

'Many things.'

'Like…'

'You are growing into a mature woman.'

'And?'

'Naturally, Alfred and I have some concerns.'

'You have spoken about me?'

'Yes.'

'What about, may I ask?'

'Your future in this country.'

'That's a broad way of looking at it.'

'Nevertheless, we still want the best for you and to ensure you don't make any mistakes, as any concerned parents would.'

'Any specifics?'

'I won't lie to you, but both Alfred and I feel the time is coming soon, if it is not here already, when you will probably want to settle down and get married to a nice young man.'

'Well, I am not surprised.'

'Alfred said both of you had spoken about it.'

'Yes, on a few occasions,' her gaze shifted from her mother to the huge apple tree of Hell House and to her secret lover, Jerome.

'That was what John spoke to you about just now?'

'Hmmm, I can see you are very observant. Yes we did. He cares about you and would do anything for you.'

'Is that so?'

'He seems troubled that there may be—'

'What? John doesn't seem to understand that love is something you can't buy. I have been real nice to him. I haven't shown him any bad face – all I have shown him is respect.'

'Then what is the problem?'

'I am not certain, Mom. I leave that to time. I won't push anything as far as John is concerned.'

'Is there someone else?' she asked, not even realising the question had slipped out of her mouth without any thought to it.

'Even if there is someone else, Mom, I don't think I want you to know until I am certain myself.'

'I understand, but it would be in the best interest of the family if we at least knew who you were going out with.'

'But I am not going out, Mom.'

'That is beside the point, my dear.'

'Regardless of that, Mom, I will spare myself the embarrassment and wait until I am certain.'

'Well, if you feel that way then there is nothing much we can do about that. Just remember there is a possible slave uprising brewing.'

'Dad at it again?'

'You must remember your father's interests and investments.'

'Those poor souls. I thought you would be more sympathetic, Mom.'

'I am, it's only that we have a lot at stake.'

'We have to look at the fact that slavery will be abolished someday.'

'Maybe, maybe not.'

'That kind of system will never last long.'

'We will see.'

'Anyway, Mom, I want you to enjoy life here – not to worry about me. I will be all right. I want you and Dad to make the best of life here and be happy.'

'We are and we want you to be too.'

'But I am. Trust me.'

Lynda smiled and gave her a hug.

★

It was the Sunday that Alice had been dreading. Jerome was at church and in a few minutes time they would be alone. She had to tell him or else life would not be the same anymore for her. Guilt would kill her. As soon as they were alone, Jerome sensed that something was wrong.

'You don't look so happy,' he said, holding her hands.

'I am not. I won't lie to you.'

'What is it?'

'It is something that is hurting me and it will probably hurt you too.'

'I am waiting.'

'It is not so easy, Jerome. Promise me you won't do anything foolish.'

'It's difficult to give you my word when I don't have the slightest clue what this is all about.'

'I am no longer a virgin.'

Jerome stared at the sky. The revelation had to come sooner or later. Somehow, she had to be unfaithful to him in the same way that he had been cheating on her.

'Who is it?' he mumbled.

'It is not like that Jerome.'

He looked at her searchingly. 'Then how?'

Alice looked down on her trembling hands, uncertain of how she should say it.

'I was raped,' she blurted out with a sob. Luckily, no one was near their little secret spot. She fell uncontrollably into Jerome's arms, wetting his shirt with tears of sorrow and discomfort.

'Raped?' his voice trembled. 'Raped? Raped? By whom?'

She hesitated.

'C'mon Alice, if you have come thus far you will have to tell me.'

'L-Larry.'

'Massa Larry?'

'Y-yes,' she stammered withdrawing her head from his chest and placing it back on it again.

'Massa Larry,' he said, trying to convince himself that it had really been him. 'How could he?'

'H-he wants me to be his sex slave.'

'What? Are you serious?'

'H-he is serious.'

'What can I do?'

'Nothing Jerome,' she sobbed aloud. 'Nothing, nothing... we could be doomed for ever.'

'I won't let this happen.'

Alice got serious. She withdrew again from his arms. 'Jerome, remember we are slaves. We have masters and until that changes there is nothing we can do.'

'Try to avoid him.'

'I already plan on doing that. He waited until no one was around and claimed he was sick in bed.'

'Miss Sarah?'

'She was in the field.'

'I see. The abolitionists are our only hope.'

'Until then?'

'We have to use our heads and see how we can get around the problem. He still has a wife and you have to use her as a shield.'

'Meaning?'

'Try to stick with her all the time. You work with her, right?'

'Yes.'

'He won't come by your bunk, so don't try to go near his.'

'But I have to make his bed each day.'

'Go in there only when Miss Sarah is around.'

'And when he pretends to be sick?'

'Tell him you have a disease.'

'What? I can't lie about sickness.'

'Which would you prefer... to be raped?'

'There isn't much choice, eh?'

'You are right,' he said, hugging her, forgetting Anita, and feeling a rage burning inside him. Larry Daniels was a marked man.

Chapter Fifteen

Anita Campbell always followed her instincts. Again, she was spot on. Maude could be more useful now than she had imagined. If there was one individual whom she should share her little secret with, then it had to be her. On the other hand, she had a gut feeling that she either suspected something, or Jerome had confided in her and told her everything.

Once Maude knew, a line of communication to Jerome could be opened for her. She hoped Maude would be in support of their relationship. What if she wasn't? She hadn't thought of that. Nevertheless, she must speak to her as a matter of urgency.

Maude was in the kitchen, washing up the dishes after an early breakfast. Anita had been watching her mood all morning. It was Maude as usual, nothing strange, nothing out of the ordinary.

'Had a good night?' Anita asked her, putting down her plate beside her.

'Uh-huh.'

'You sound sleepy.'

'I am always sleepy, Miss Anita.'

'You deserve a long rest.'

'What can we do? We are here to work.'

Anita's head bowed in disgust. She looked at Maude with a sad face. 'You know I pray to God it will be all over soon. I know Dad has a lot at stake but it is not right.'

'I know your feelings ma'am. You are the only true

friend around here.'

Anita came closer to her and touched her arm, then gripped it tightly. 'I will always be there for you all,' she said with a smile.

'You are very kind Miss Anita; you will be a good wife someday.'

'A good wife!' she exclaimed.

'Yes Miss Anita, a good wife.'

'Poor me.'

'You are rich.'

'That's true but a good husband doesn't just drop from the sky.'

'Jerome would make a good husband if—'

Anita put her hands over her mouth in amazement. She was speechless, she was dumb, yet she was happy and felt victorious. 'Y-y-you k-know about…'

'Yes Miss Anita, he told me, even though I suspected long before.'

'Shhh,' she said, putting her hand over Maude's mouth. 'It must remain a secret between the three of us.'

'Four.'

'Wh-who? Somebody else knows?'

'Yes.'

'Who?' she asked, nervously.

'Don't worry, it's safe.'

'Babwe?'

'Who else.'

'Y'know, I feel real happy.'

'I know you love him. The look on your face when he is around is enough. But Miss Anita you have to be very careful. Your father, John and Miss Lynda…'

'Do you like her?'

'We talked.'

'Talked? About what?'

'You.'

'Me?'

'Yes. She wanted to know what has been happening in your life.'

'And?'

'Well, I told her I didn't know much except to say you are a fine girl who deserves a fine young man, which is scarce in these parts.'

Anita came up and hugged her tightly, Maude's fleshy body almost flattening her out. 'You are my second mother Maude,' she said, withdrawing from her grasp.

'Jerome is my son and in a way you are my daughter.'

'I would want to be your daughter-in-law if things were right.'

'We have hope my dear that someday soon slavery will be no more.'

'Have you heard anything recently?'

'In Spanish Town the other day, there was talk that plantations are being burnt and that things are moving fast.'

'Really?' she said, a little concerned now.

'It could come sooner than imagined.'

'My father is worried. I guess I am too, in one sense, and in the other I could be the happiest girl around.'

Maude thought of Alice. She too was a nice girl and could be the happiest around but only after Jerome got some of Anita's money. She hated that thought, but she saw that as a kind of repayment for all the wrongs that had been done to them. She wouldn't want to see Anita hurt. Truly, she was like a daughter. Maude could only leave everything to time. Maybe the uncertainties would work themselves out in due course. If there was one thing Maude had to do, it was to encourage both Alice and Anita about Jerome. In the final analysis, only one would be the winner. Someone had to lose and for the moment, she was not concerned about that.

'Let us pray things will work out soon.'

'That's a thought.'

'I do that every night. I pray to Massa God to end our plight. I go to church every Sunday and I pray about that.'

'Do you think it might be a good idea for me to visit your church?'

Maude's thoughts quickly flashed to Alice and she saw trouble. 'Hmmm, to be honest with you Miss Anita I don't think that is a good idea.'

'Any particular reason?'

'No. Only that slaves...'

'All around?'

'Yes, and it would not look right.'

'But isn't it the same God we worship?'

'Yes,' she said sitting on a wooden bench in the kitchen. The dishes were all done.

Anita sat beside her. 'Okay, I understand. It's just that I rarely see Jerome.'

'I know. What can I do?'

That was the statement of the morning. That was what she wanted to hear. 'You really mean that Maude?'

'Remember, I want to help as long as you two are very careful.'

'Don't worry. We are.'

'Then it is no problem for me.'

'I want to see him tonight,' she said calmly, waiting for her reaction.

'Where? When?' said Maude.

'The usual place... Hell House.'

'Hell House? That is so near.'

'Okay, Lookout.'

'Have you ever met him at Hell House?'

'Twice.'

Maude's eyes widened in fright. 'Miss Anita, p-please don't... never again.'

'You are right. That could be dangerous.'

'Lookout is much better.'

Tell him midnight. That is the only time he can work by.'

'That will be fine, Miss Anita. That will be fine.'

Lynda walked into the kitchen in riding clothes. 'Hey what are you two up to?'

'Just talking about how to manage when we don't have a clock.'

'Oh; well I am going for my Monday morning ride. Would you like to come, Anita?'

'Sure. Why not? I am going to get ready. See you Maude.'

'Bye, Miss Anita.'

Lynda followed her through the door, somehow feeling somewhat relieved that she had decided to go riding with her.

★

John wanted to see Anita badly. He didn't even bother to shout and yell at the slaves this morning. His thoughts were somewhere else – Anita's bedroom.

Jerome's eyes never left him. At one point, he almost laughed aloud when he thought of the night he had hit him very hard. That was sweet revenge.

John took his break under a tree, eyes never leaving the slaves. He did not hear the horses come up the trail behind him.

'Having a good day?' shouted Lynda.

John turned quickly to see the two women getting out of their saddles. 'Oh, hi, Lynda. Anita I am so delighted to see you.' He went over to help Anita who was still trying to touch the ground. 'Here let me help you.'

'Thanks John,' she said, holding his hand briefly.

'Much obliged.'

'How's the day?' Lynda asked again.

'It is going all right. Those bums are moving nicely along. These canes are not so big like the previous batch.'

'I see. Let me see how big they are,' said Lynda, walking towards the nearest pile. Anita sensed that her mother wanted her to be alone with John, at least for a few minutes. John welcomed the opportunity.

'So how have you been keeping?' he said, as soon as Lynda had stepped away.

'I am all right.'

'I haven't been seeing much of you lately.'

'I am at home trying to adjust to having Mother around.'

'She's a fine woman.'

'You think so?'

'Oh yes. Alfred is a lucky man. I wish I were that lucky.'

'Hmm.'

John was hoping for a better reaction. 'When are we going to start seeing more of each other?' he asked.

'I don't know.'

'How about tonight?'

Anita trembled a little. 'Tonight? No... I-I have a good book I want to read and would prefer to be alone.'

'I understand. Many nights, that is all I have to keep me company.'

'I think I'd better go and look at the canes too,' she said walking away.

'How about tomorrow?'

'To be honest, John, I have a lot of adjustment to do with Mom around and I need a little more time to sort things out.'

'How much time will you need?' he said.

Anita sensed a tinge of anger in his voice but she couldn't care less. If that was the final conversation with him as far as their relationship was concerned then she would have been a very happy woman. John's presence had begun to irritate her, it was like a thorn in the side.

'All the time I can get John.' She walked away, leaving him standing there only to bring into focus a figure that resembled Jerome in the far corner, slashing away at the tall cane plants.

John was angry. No longer than tonight could he wait to carry out the first phase of his plan.

If the slaves had overheard the conversation between Anita and John they would have known the reason for John's anger for the remainder of the afternoon. He yelled and swore all afternoon, calling them names he had never even used before.

The only person who had an inclination of what might have transpired was Jerome. He didn't see Anita walking away from John but was taken aback when he saw her standing beside her mother only about a minute after Lynda had left them both. Babwe was busy on the other side of field and could not see what had been happening.

John could hardly wait for the sun to vanish from the horizon. He quickly went to his room, took a bath, put on some fresh clothes, had something to eat, and then sat in his chair for a moment of relaxation. Later on he had to go out to fulfil part of his plan.

John was dead beat. He fell asleep and must have slept for nearly four hours – too late for what he had planned.

He jumped quickly to his feet and lurched towards the window. He looked towards the house of his boss and could see that there was light, a pale one, in the living room area.

John rushed through the door. Anita must still be up reading. Was it too late for a conversation on what she had read? Or would it be too late to enter her bedroom?

John walked quietly up the steps at the front of the house. The light looked even paler now. He tried the lock and to his surprise, the door opened. What the heck? he thought.

No one was in the living room. John stepped in, looking around like a thief. No one was around. He tiptoed up the stairs towards Anita's bedroom. At least if someone came in he had an excuse in that he had seen the light and found the door open. He reached the door of Anita's room. It was closed but he decided to try it. It, too, was open. Inside: as dark as a dungeon. Was she in there? John edged towards the white curtain and parted it a little in order to get some more light from the half moon. Fortunately, the glare shone directly on the bed. It was empty. 'What is going on?' he mumbled. He hated to think of the possibilities.

He tiptoed out of the room, back down the stairs and out through the door. Outside, he looked in every direction but the darkness of the night made matters worse. He didn't see anything.

John walked down the steps towards Hell House. Under the tree, he stopped to look around but again, saw nothing. At that moment something startled his ear. He heard footsteps. Turning quickly in the direction of Lookout, John could discern a figure moving in his direction. He dodged behind the trunk of the tree in order not to be seen.

Within a few seconds the figure, which he easily recognised as that of Anita, passed him at a crawling pace. She had her arms folded and was walking as if she was in no hurry. John wanted to make his presence known but decided against that.

What was she doing out so late at night and alone? John intended to find out.

Chapter Sixteen

What a night. What a rendezvous she had at Lookout last night with the man in her life. There would be many more now that their little secret was out but limited to only two other people.

Anita had been sleeping all morning. Now, it was almost midday. She sat on the veranda reading a book her mother had bought for her.

John's timing was right. He couldn't wait any longer to have another chat with her in light of last night's puzzling discovery. John had left a supervisor in charge so that he could come and see Anita.

'Is that the book you were telling me about?' he asked, as he rode up against the veranda.

'Yes, it is,' she said dryly.

'Didn't bother to read last night, eh?'

Anita looked at him, wondering if he was sniffing around for something.

'I did, but not for long.'

'I see. It is better to read in the days, the light is much better than at nights.'

'That is true.'

'What are you doing tonight? Anything special?'

'I think I will go to bed early.'

'You were up late last night?'

Anita looked at him again. 'As a matter of fact I was.'

'I was too. I couldn't sleep.'

'I felt like going for a walk and I did just that.'

'Really? You should have let me know and we could have gone together.'

'I didn't really need any company.'

John came closer to her. 'Anita, you have to be careful, lots of things are going on out there; you shouldn't be alone out there at night. Did your father know?'

'No. I saw no reason to tell him.'

'Next time you should probably let him know in the event that something happens.'

'I was in no rush to come home. I enjoyed every moment of it and I had no fear that anything would happen.'

'Where did you go?'

'Why all these questions, John? I am a big girl, remember? I can take care of myself.' She didn't want to say that but she thought John was going a bit too far.

'You know I care about you, Anita.'

'That doesn't change anything John. I appreciate your concern but I will be okay.'

John realised he was getting nowhere and he decided against carrying the conversation any further. 'All right, as you wish, but just remember I still care about you, despite the fact that there seems to be a bridge slowly building between us.'

'A bridge?'

'Don't you see, or are you refusing to see?'

'I am sorry but I don't know what you are getting at.'

'We don't have enjoyable conversations any more. We don't go anywhere. We don't enjoy each other's company. What is wrong, Anita?'

'Something probably is wrong.'

John wanted to hold her hands; would she allow it? That chance he wouldn't take because of the direction the conversation was now heading.

'If something is wrong, it is not from my point of view.'

Anita felt like telling it like it was. 'Maybe it is me then.'

'Are you trying to tell me something?'

'You could interpret it that way.'

'What is it then?' he asked, anxiety in his voice.

Anita hesitated for a while. She must come out with it now, right now. It would make things easier for her. 'Honestly John. You are a nice man.'

'You really mean that?'

'Yes, but...'

'But what?'

'It won't work.'

John's heart had raced a little only seconds ago. Now it appeared as if it had come to a standstill. 'Why Anita, why? It can if we only give it a chance.'

'I never wanted to get into anything serious from the beginning. I only wanted company and you were good at that, John. And I appreciate that, but to have or enter into an intimate relationship is not what I am interested in.'

John was dumb struck, although he had expected to hear something like that.

'You used me!' he snapped. Anger was in his voice as well as in the way he moved his hands.

'No John. Don't look at it like that. You were a good friend and still are.'

'Friend? That is the way you look at it,' he snapped again.

'Honestly, that was the way I saw it and it doesn't make sense to pretend about it. Dad and Mom want us to be together but I told them it wouldn't work.'

'They will be disappointed.'

'They knew it wouldn't work.'

'Are you certain about that?'

'Yes, because I told them.'

John was tempted to ask her if there was someone else. But who? There could be no one else. He would have known. Last night; was she with someone? He must continue his investigation. That would be the only way to get some satisfactory answers to his most pressing question. Was Anita seeing someone else?

'I will still care for you, Anita. As long as I live you will be in my heart.'

'You will always be a special friend, John. And I hope from now on there is no strain on our relationship.'

'I won't promise anything because it is not a nice feeling to know that someone you care about is not thinking the way you would expect. I will try my best.' With that, he jumped into the saddle and rode away.

Anita saw anger all over him. She felt sad; but on the other hand she was relieved. It was like a heavy load had been removed from her head. Her thoughts turned to Jerome.

⋆

Jerome had watched John mount his horse and ride towards Jack's Place. About half an hour later he came back. It must have been the first time Jerome had ever seen him leave at lunchtime. It was something urgent. He wondered if something had gone wrong last night.

On the way home, he told Babwe of his fears.

'I wouldn't worry about that,' said Babwe.

' Anita is too smart to let anything happen, I know, but you can't help but worry.'

'There are other things to worry about.'

'I know. For instance, Alice. What should I do about an animal like Larry?'

'Leave him to time.'

'The abolition movement or Massa God?'

'Both.'

'He is going to try again.'

'Maybe. Alice will have to try hard not to allow him.'

'I have already told her that.'

'Good. My son, everything will be all right. What you should be worrying about is the day when you will have to chose between them.'

Instantaneously, Jerome became worried. He feared that day. With every moment he spent with Anita, the situation became more complicated. Since Alice had been raped it made matters worse. He sympathised with her and felt he should be a kind of guide for her; yet whenever he thought of the soft and tender body of Anita he became a weak person ready to submit to the demands of a white woman.

'Let us not talk about that, Babwe. When the time comes I will decide. Let us hope that I am a free man by then.'

'I am confident we could all be.'

*

Maude was happy that Anita had organised another trip to Malvern. She would be taking her mother with her. And as expected, the usual three would go with her. They had little notice, Anita wanted to leave earlier but couldn't. She wanted to spend two nights in Malvern but again she failed to convince Alfred to do that. Her father was worried about a spate of fires which had become commonplace all over the parish. Fortunately, there had been none in Big Yard, so far.

They left early Friday morning at the first break of day. Lynda welcomed the trip. The clothes she had brought with her from England were too much for the tropical climate. She needed a whole new wardrobe. Alfred didn't object to that; he was only concerned about their safety.

'Don't you worry Massa Alfred. I will take care of them,' Babwe assured him as they rode away in the buggy.

'I know I can depend on good ol' Babwe,' he grinned.

It was a relief for Anita to get away from there, get away

from John and have in her presence the slave of her dream and his forbidden love.

At daybreak there was no sun. Dark nimbus clouds hung like stalactites in the eastern sky. Without a doubt, it could start raining soon. Had they seen that before they left, Alfred would have convinced them to postpone the trip. Anita didn't want that. She wanted to go regardless of the weather. Babwe saw her looking in the direction of the clouds.

'Don't worry, ma'am, I don't think the rain will catch us today.'

'It is not looking good,' said Lynda.

'The rain will go up along the coast but we are moving away from the coast,' grinned Babwe.

'You seem to know about the weather,' she replied.

'He has been predicting it for many years,' said Anita. Jerome remained silent. He knew it was customary for slaves to be quiet unless spoken to by their masters. If Lynda was not around they could talk freely. Babwe was what you could call a senior slave. Even though he was a slave, he was allowed to do certain things because of his age and usefulness as well as wit.

'I take it we won't get wet then,' said Lynda, looking around at Maude for a comment.

'I guarantee you Babwe knows what he is talking about,' Maude assured her.

'How long have you been with us?' Lynda asked.

'Must have been about as far back as I can remember,' Babwe said.

'How about you Maude?'

The look on Lynda's face reminded Maude so much of her daughter. 'About the same,' Maude laughed.

'How about that young man?' Lynda said, pointing to Jerome.

'That is Jerome – my son,' said Maude proudly. 'His

father was sent away when he was young; his mother died a few years ago and I look after him. A good boy. He was born on the plantation and there isn't anything in this world I wouldn't do for him.'

'He looks strong. I am sure he works very hard.'

'I feel very safe when he's around, Mom,' said Anita, a broad smile erupting on her sleepy face.

'Has he been to Malvern with you?'

'A few times, and I tell you, he has done a good job, along with Babwe, in making me feel safe.'

'Good; then he will go anywhere we go.'

That was just what Anita wanted to hear.

Chapter Seventeen

John Stewart was no longer a happy man. It had all happened so quickly. It was only a few days ago he was on top of the world; he had been living in dreamland, but reality had wakened him from that dream. Anita had finally dropped the bombshell he had feared all along. What should he do next?

John had attempted the other night to prove something. He didn't succeed. Now he wondered if he had been close to something. Should he try again? He was now convinced he should; the only reason for that thought was the uneasiness he felt with Anita's late night walk. Was there something else behind it?

Alfred would be alone tonight. He must seize the opportunity to have a talk with him. He was sitting beside the window when John walked in unannounced.

'Hi – thought I'd drop by to keep you company.'

'Oh, that's all right. I was thinking about getting off to bed.'

'So early?'

'With Lynda and Anita away what better time to get an early rest?'

'I guess you are right.'

'You are missing Anita too?'

John sat down in a chair beside him, both hands pressed to his knees like those men getting on in age. 'That's exactly what I came to talk to you about.'

'Something wrong?'

John paused for a few seconds, a stern look coming across his face. 'We had a talk.'

'And?'

'She said there was nothing to our relationship.'

'Just like that?'

'Yep, she doesn't even want to give it a try.'

'Did she give any reasons?'

'Well, she said we were only friends; she didn't want it, or didn't see it any further than that.'

Alfred was disappointed and John could hear it in his voice, but he knew there was nothing he could do.

'As much as I would have wanted to see the two of you together, John, and you know that, there is nothing I can really do.'

'I know that, Alfred.'

'What will you do now?'

'I can only keep looking around until Mrs Right comes along.'

'But do you think, as I have asked before, that she may be interested in someone else?'

'I often wonder about that, but if she is seeing someone else, who?'

'That's the question. There are no other eligible men within ten miles of here. What about Malvern?'

'Malvern?'

'Yes, she has gone there a few times, especially in the last two months. I wonder if she is seeing someone there?' Alfred asked, almost certain now that he could be right.

'You know, I have never thought about that.'

'When Lynda returns I will ask her for some details about Anita's activities there.'

'Good,' said John, grinning for the first time since the dialogue began. 'That could be the answer to my question.'

★

Anita had never had a more pleasurable moment with Jerome than she had just had, only fifteen minutes ago. She lay sprawled on her back, listening to her mother's loud snore. Apparently, she hadn't even changed her sleeping position since Anita had crept out of the room. The journey had surely knocked her out and, not being accustomed to such rigorous travel, she was really dead beat.

They had ridden into Malvern at sunset. Lynda wanted to go straight to bed without even eating. Anita liked that and wasted no time in getting her dinner and seeing to it that the slaves had their fill too. When she had taken up dinner for Lynda she wasn't surprised to hear her snores.

Anita quickly cleaned herself up and boldly walked out of the room down to the back of the hotel where the slaves were bunking for the night. Maude and Babwe were fast asleep but the twinkling eye of Jerome greeted her in lust and awe.

*

Alice was wishing that Friday night had been Saturday night instead. It would have been one more day nearer to Sunday – church day.

She yearned for Jerome's presence. He had been so angry at their last meeting. By now, she anticipated, his anger towards Larry must have subsided. Alice couldn't blame Jerome for feeling that way. At least, if he cared no lesser reaction was to be expected.

Alice got down on her knees before going to bed and prayed to Massa God for deliverance – from slavery and from the adulterous hands of Larry Daniels. She prayed that she and Jerome could get married soon.

Sunday morning came with a golden tint. Alice got up a little earlier than usual. She also left a little earlier for church, more than anxious to see Jerome. But to her chagrin, even after one hour following the service, there was no Jerome. Alice wanted to go over to see Maude and possibly Jerome. To do that, she had to get permission from Larry; he was the last person she wanted to see. In order not to get too worried, she concluded that Jerome must have had a really hard week and was probably getting some rest. Alice was confident she would see him next Sunday.

*

Jerome could hardly get up out of his bed Monday morning. The weekend trip to Malvern took its toll on him. He didn't get back until late Sunday afternoon. While he didn't get to say much to Anita, he had two full nights of her. She was making up for all that time they had missed. Jerome wondered how she could have slipped out of her room unnoticed and felt uneasy at first. She had whispered in his ears that her mother was dead to the world.

Jerome remembered the whisper in his dream and was awakened by another whisper, this time for real, from Babwe.

'It is Monday morning,' he said simply. Jerome sprang to his feet to look into the sleepy eyes of Babwe, half grinning.

It was very hot and humid in the field. Jerome was barely moving the machete; all his energy was drained on the journey and those two nights he spent with Anita. The thought of what had happened then must have been the only thing that kept him going. But unfortunately, his lethargic performance was not going unnoticed. It caught the eyes of John.

'You lazy wretch,' John snapped. He approached him with a small whip in his hand.

Jerome didn't expect him to use it and he didn't. However, the sentence that was coming would be the usual cruel one.

'You will be going to Hell House for the next two nights.' He said nothing more.

The thought of Hell House had brought back some pleasant memories for Jerome and now he wondered if his punishment would be a treat.

Babwe heard the sentence and he, too, thought that probably it would be an opportunity for Jerome to meet Anita. Babwe knew they had met there already and from what Jerome told him, it was one heck of a time they had. Poor Jerome, Babwe grinned inwardly; he was a loser in whatever way you looked at the whole situation.

★

Alfred was happy to have his family back with him.

'Had a good trip?' he asked, his eyes moving from Lynda to Anita, as they sat down for supper.

'It was well worth it,' said Lynda.

'Mom slept so deep. She was really tired.'

'I did enjoy the outing, though. Malvern seems to be a nice little town and sells some good and attractive things too.'

'How about you Anita – did you enjoy yourself?' he asked, more interested in her answer.

'It couldn't have been better. I am glad Mom got some rest and that she got some nice clothes suitable for this climate.'

'The clothes are a little different from those in England but they will do.'

'You had a full day to shop, you didn't have time for going to the circus usually there at this time of the year?'

'Circus? We only passed it. Mom was so taken up with the clothes that by the time we finished getting the food, it was supper time.'

'I see.'

'Next time we can probably spend two days.'

'Anita, while you were gone John and I had a talk.'

Lynda looked around at Anita as if something had gone wrong. 'Is something wrong?' she asked.

'It is finished, if ever there was something?' Alfred mused.

'Anita; I thought you and John were getting closer.'

'That is just a thought Mom – nothing else. John and I were only friends.'

'Couldn't you give it some time?'

'John wanted that.'

'And?'

'I told him it would be a waste of time. I have no feelings for him in that regard.'

'Don't you think time could have proven otherwise?

Anita stopped eating as the others had. 'I am sure it would not have made a difference.'

'How could you be so certain about that?'

'I have proven it over and over again.'

'How?' asked Lynda.

'Well Mom. I was so lonely that at one point I was forcing myself to believe that John could turn out to be the right one for me. However, I soon realised that I was wrong all along. John is a nice man but he is not my type.'

'Do you see any of your type around here?' Alfred quickly asked.

Anita fumbled for words. How should she answer such a question? Did the two judges before her have something up their sleeves?

'Not really,' she said dryly.

'Have you met any lately?' Alfred asked again.

'Is this an interrogation?' Anita responded.

'No my dear,' said Lynda, placing her hands over

Anita's. 'We want the best for you and you know that.'

'Then am I not free to chose on my own?'

'Of course, my dear, but you know how parents are; they want the best for their children, especially if there is only one, and moreover, if it is a daughter.'

Anita blushed. 'I know your concerns but there is nothing you have to worry about. I am mature enough to know what is best for me.'

'We know you are; however, we want to be assured that you are choosing the right someone,' Alfred said.

'John is a nice guy and we only thought that if the two of you could get together then we would have nothing to worry about.'

'Mom, I agree that John is a nice man. H-he is not my type at all and to be honest with you, I don't think I would be happy with him for the rest of my life.'

'And you are certain about that?'

'Of course, Mom.'

'There aren't many young men around these parts, dear, and it seems as though you will be waiting for a long time to get one that suits you,' remarked Alfred.

'I have been thinking about that too, Alfred, and that is part of the concern we have for you, dear.'

'Don't you worry about that, everything will turn out to be fine. You may get a surprise one day.'

'Let us hope that we won't have to wait too long,' said Alfred. 'I can hardly wait to see my grandchildren. Time is moving fast, Anita.'

Almost immediately, Anita remembered the passionate moments with Jerome. She had carefully chosen every one of those encounters to fall at the time they did. There was nothing to worry about.

'When I am tired of waiting we will probably send you to England to find one,' grinned Lynda.

'Mom, that you won't have to I can assure you. Be patient and everything will work out fine.'

At that moment, somehow Lynda and Alfred wanted to believe her and in fact they did, to a certain extent.

Chapter Eighteen

Hell House was living up to its reputation tonight. It had been hell for Jerome, so far. The mosquitoes never gave him a chance; the last two hours were spent trying to catch the insects as they sang into his ears. Jerome was annoyed and he had a right to be. He was being bitten all over.

But relief came somewhere around midnight. Anita marched under the tree with that precious blanket in her hand. She ran into his shackled arms and kissed him hard.

'I can't stay for long,' she mumbled between kisses. 'Dad is still up. I managed to slip out of the house.'

'Go, quickly!' Jerome said abruptly. 'Come back tomorrow night, I will be here.'

Anita released him reluctantly and ran towards the house. She slipped behind the door she had left unlocked and was strolling across the living room, when she saw Alfred coming down the stairs. She was frightened.

'Hey, where are you coming from?' he queried.

'Oh, I-I went outside for some fresh air,' a little trembling in her voice.

'Anita, you are getting me worried. A lot of things are happening out there. You shouldn't go out alone.'

'But Dad I was only on the steps.'

'Wherever – houses are being burnt and plantations are being raided.'

'Yet nothing is happening, eh?'

'I didn't want you to get worried Anita but the truth is things are really moving fast The freedom fighters are

144

serious about abolishing slavery.'

'You mean slavery could soon be stopped?'

'I hate to admit that. The latest word from Spanish Town is that slavery could be abolished as early as next year.'

'What? That early?'

'Yes. That's why I wanted or hoped you would have settled down with John, in the event that we lose out on our investment.'

Fear gripped Anita's faces yet she was pleased in another sense. 'I don't think that will happen, Dad.'

'Maybe not, but please, Anita don't go out alone. You understand?'

'As you wish, Dad. Good night. Go and get some rest now.'

'I will.'

Strange. Going for a walk after midnight? Alfred thought. He must speak with John tomorrow.

*

Alice was relieved that Larry hadn't been bothering her since the recent incident. In fact he stayed far from her. She had been convinced that he was going to try again whenever she was tidying up the master's bedroom. So far, so good. She hoped it stayed that way.

Jerome would be in church on Sunday. Alice was reassured by Elizabeth, Maude's close friend. On learning that Jerome had gone to Malvern with the new mistress, Alice was relieved that he had been absent from church for a good reason. She longed for him now; she yearned to feel his touch. Notwithstanding all of that, she could not help wondering if Jerome had eyes for any other young slave girl in the neighbourhood. The church was no exception, there were quite a few of them around on Sundays. Was he watching secretly?

*

The first thing that was on Alfred's agenda for Tuesday morning was to go and visit John. After breakfast, he mounted his horse and rode towards the field. Maude watched him as he gulped down his breakfast in a flash. Why the rush? she wondered. Maude's eyes followed him through the doors and out to the stables. She watched him mount the stallion and ride in the direction of the field Jerome was working. Did the visit have anything to do with Jerome, Hell House, or Anita? It had to be, she assumed.

John saw Alfred coming and he knew it must be something urgent. Any time that Alfred visited him, it had to be important. What could the visit be all about? He was anxious.

'How's it going,' Alfred said, riding up beside John.

'All right, I guess. We got off to a good start.'

'Will we take off this crop on time?'

'Oh, sure we will.'

'I hope we can because the reports from Spanish Town aren't good.'

'More trouble?'

'Yes. There is speculation now that slavery could be abolished as early as next year. Some plantations are losing money and I only hope we can get off this harvest before all the trouble begins.'

'Don't worry, we will.'

'Was there anything unusual around here last night?' he said, dismounting from the horse.

'No, why?'

'I don't know what to make of this...'

'What?'

'I saw Anita coming through the door shortly after midnight.'

John's eyes twinkled either in disappointment or with relief that his puzzle might finally be on the way to being solved. 'Really? Midnight? What was her excuse?'

'She said she just went out on the steps for some fresh air.'

'That could be so.'

'But at midnight?'

'Yeah, you have a point, but there was nothing unusual,' he said scratching his heads 'except for...'

'For what?'

'No, forget it. That's irrelevant.' John would have preferred if Alfred didn't know about it, especially at a time when slaves were getting violent in some areas.

'What? Let me hear about it.'

'A slave was at Hell House last night.'

'Why?'

'He was wasting time.'

'Who?'

John hesitated. 'The young slave who went with you to Spanish Town.'

'Jerome?' Alfred's eyes widened, fearing what such an assumption could lead to. He stared past John out into the field where the slaves were slashing away at the cane plants. The mass of black bodies shining in the sun was hard to distinguish. Jerome was among them; that was all he knew.

Alfred scratched his beard and repeated the name.

'He went to Spanish Town, Malvern twice.'

'And to Junction with Anita and me.'

Alfred made a step forward and then turned around to look at John in disbelief. 'Did Anita... in fact, Anita was so defensive over this slave going with her...'

'Aah, I think we are on to something,' said John.

'It can't be,' Alfred snapped angrily.' 'My daughter being

involved with a slave. It can't be! No way.'

'It could jolly well be Alfred. Some women are unpredictable.'

'It seems possible now but for the time being I will refuse to accept that.'

'Looking back now, I can remember previous conversations with her and she was so much in favour of their welfare. She felt we were being too harsh.'

'Can you send back that slave to Hell House tonight?'

'It is already booked.' John grinned.

'Can you monitor from the outside?'

'I will.'

'Good. I will from the inside.' Alfred jumped on his horse in a rage and rode back towards the house.

Jerome heard the sound of hooves and looked out towards the tree they had been talking under. A rather unusual visit, he thought.

Maude didn't hear Alfred come through the front door and it wasn't until she overheard the conversation with Lynda in his study that she realised that he had come back. She crept up beside the door in time to hear Alfred say '…he went to Malvern twice with her, to Junction and to Spanish Town. What do you think?'

'Let's not jump to any conclusions,' Lynda was saying. 'I don't think our daughter could be so foolish as to fall in love with a slave… though I must admit that the slave is a strikingly handsome young man.'

'Huh, so you are admiring him too.'

'C'mon honey, nothing like that. Don't you know him?'

'I have seen him a few times, yes.'

'Let's keep our eyes peeled.'

Maude heard footsteps behind her. She darted from her position and was returning to the kitchen when she bumped into Anita. Wide-eyed from the encounter, Maude yanked Anita by the arm and led her into the kitchen.

'Miss Anita, your father suspects you and Jerome,' she whispered.

'What? How?'

'I don't know. I heard him talking to Miss Lynda.'

'Saying what?'

'That Jerome went to Malvern twice, Junction and Spanish Town, and that you couldn't be so foolish to fall in love with a slave.'

Anita was frightened because it was clear to her that they were discussing their relationship. 'What am I going to do?' she mumbled.

'I don't know. They aren't certain. They only suspect you.'

'I was planning to see him tonight.'

'You know you can't. You will probably have to stop seeing him for a while.'

'I wish I could. If I don't see him at least twice a week I feel like I am going crazy.'

'You have no choice now.'

'I know. Please don't say anything to Jerome – he will panic and probably even want to end the relationship.'

Maude thought for a while.

'I hate to do this to him but I think it might be the best thing right now.'

'I think so too, I will take care of everything.'

Maude wanted to believe her.

At dinner, Alfred and Anita said little. When Lynda joined them, it didn't make things any better. Anita knew the reason; however, she pretended that everything was fine.

'Have you finished that book you were reading?' asked Lynda.

'Almost.'

'You have been reading it for a little while.'

'I am taking my time. It is so interesting that I hardly

want to come to the end.'

'I see.'

'Have you heard anything further about the abolition movement, Dad?'

'No,' he said dryly, trying to hide his anger.

'Don't pray too much for that day to come,' said Lynda.

'What do you mean by that, Mom?' She stared at her.

'I mean it is a day we should all be dreading.'

'Oh.' Anita was giggling inside.

'You know what? I am going to bed early tonight,' said Alfred.

'Me too, I am tired from that Malvern trip. It's like I still haven't recovered,' said Lynda smiling. 'How do you do it?' she asked Anita.

'I sort of get used to it,' she said.

Smart girl, Alfred said in his mind as he got up from the table. Really smart, but how long will she be smart for, probably not after tonight, he thought.

'Have a good night my dear,' said Lynda.

'I will, Mom, I think I will sleep early too,' she said, and she knew she had to do that unwillingly.

Anita sat alone at the table for a while. Right out there, only a few yards away from where she was sitting, was the love of her life, sitting in the coolness of the night providing blood for mosquitoes. She collected the blanket she gave him last night. By the time she had reached there he was already up and waiting for her to retrieve it. Tonight, he was expecting the same treatment; unfortunately he wouldn't get it, and he would be disappointed. She got up and looked through the window. Outside was all black. Tears came to her eyes and she really felt like going out there. She knew she couldn't take any chance whatsoever. She owed their relationship that much.

She couldn't stand the thought anymore, so Anita headed up the stairs and went straight to her bed in tears.

Her pillow became wet within a few minutes. The sobs were silent and real, and they lingered until she fell asleep.

Alfred and Lynda heard her door slam. They wanted to be certain she didn't come out again for the rest of the night. They kept guard in a lightless living room and stayed there until about two o'clock before they were convinced she wouldn't leave her bedroom, at least for that night.

Outside, John made his bed on a bench along the side of the stone-built stairway. The bench could only be seen when the stairs were descended and someone was walking out to the other end of the house. John stayed there until about two thirty and then called it a night. Were they all wrong? Alfred and Lynda wished they were. John wasn't certain about his position.

Chapter Nineteen

Jerome was relieved that he was back in his bed again. The room was a little cosy, probably because he hadn't slept in it for the past two nights. His absence from it made him appreciate it more.

He lay sprawled on his back, trying to relax but finding it difficult because of his bewilderment over Anita's failure to show up last night. Jerome felt like he had become addicted to her and her passionate moments. He wanted to resist her but that was becoming more and more difficult each time he saw her.

Jerome's thoughts were interrupted by shouts coming from a narrow track beside their sleeping quarters. He jumped to his feet, opened the wooden window and peered into the black night. Surprisingly, the night was not so dark as he had anticipated.

A section of the western sky was lit up as bright as ever. It had to be a fire. He shifted his glance in the direction of the shouts and saw a couple of torches twinkling as they moved closer. The shouts were audible now. 'Fire! Fire! Fire!' came the startling voices he could easily recognise as those of children.

Jerome, who already had on his pants, reached for his shirt and ran to the other rooms, waking up everybody. 'Fire, fire: Massa Daniels' place burning down!' Within moments, everyone was on their feet, including Maude and Babwe.

Jerome ran outside and went to Alfred's front door. By

his estimate, it could be around ten o'clock, but whether Alfred was awake or not, it didn't really matter to him. There was a crisis, and with the interest Alfred had been showing in the move towards the abolition of slavery, he would definitely be interested to know what had been going on at his neighbour's.

Jerome pounded the door loudly. When he stopped he heard footsteps coming towards it. The door was opened quickly and right there, Jerome was staring into the eyes of his lover. The stare was short-lived because before he could utter a word, Alfred and Lynda came up behind her.

'What is the matter boy?' Alfred growled.

'F-fire suh, fire.'

'Fire?' all three said in unison.

'Yes suh, Massa Larry place is burning down.'

They all rushed to the window that faced the direction of Larry's plantation.

A bright glow in the dark sky greeted their eyes. Alfred and Lynda rushed upstairs. John must have heard the noise and he came in at the very moment Anita was walking back to the door where Jerome had been standing.

John walked around him, examining him like an inspector. He wanted to yell at him and asked how he could be so presumptuous as to be in his master's house.

'What do you know about this fire, boy?' he too growled.

'Nuthing, suh, I heard the noise… the shouts from the children and came out and saw it.'

'Where are the children now?' asked Anita.

'Aunt Maude is taking care of them.'

Anita was trying to avoid John, however, she realised that under the circumstances it would be difficult.

Alfred was coming back down the stairs, putting on a shirt at the same time. 'Come John, we have to go and give a hand, maybe there is something we can save.' He was walking towards the door. 'Get a few other slaves and come with me,' he told Jerome.

Anita didn't wait to hear the next comment; she rushed towards her room to change her clothes. John thought she was going back to bed, so he followed Alfred.

At the Daniels' plantation, Larry and Sarah were in a frenzy. They were running from the barn to the stables trying to pour as many buckets of water as they could. A few yards away, a section of the cane field was quickly being eaten away by the flames. Slaves, from the young to the old, were up and about passing buckets and collecting buckets.

Alice was not left out of the picture. In fact, she was right up front along with Sarah, pitching water as fast as the buckets came.

They were soon joined by slaves from Jack's Place, led by Alfred and John. Lynda and Anita didn't hesitate to join the throng.

It didn't take them long to realise that there was little they could do to save the barn and stable. They didn't even attempt to do anything about the cane field. That was not so important because the canes were almost ready to be reaped. It was harvest time.

The severity of the heat forced them to move away from the inferno as far as possible. They stood motionless and watched the buildings crumble under the vicious flames.

'I had a funny feeling this would happen to me,' said Larry to Alfred.

'With what has been happening it had to come sooner or later. If it wasn't you, it would have been me,' said Alfred.

'Those wretches,' John snarled. 'I surely hope we don't have any of them on these plantations here.'

'I am confident whoever did this was not from here,' said Larry.

'How can you be so sure?' asked Alfred.

'Put it this way. I know my slaves. I treat them well and

regardless of what has been happening out there, I don't think… I don't honestly think any of them would have done that.'

'I could never swear for a slave,' John said, remembering what had happened to him recently on the lawn at Jack's Place. Could he have surprised someone who was attempting to try something?

Anita's eyes searched the well-lit surroundings for Jerome but he was nowhere around. She saw Maude and Babwe but not the man in her life. As she was about to give up something, at least a figure, at the other end of where everyone was congregated, caught her eyes. It was Jerome all right but he had company. He was talking to a girl, a young girl, and now she remembered her from the Malvern visit. A streak of jealousy ran through her stomach. Then she felt a rage building inside her. She wanted to march over there to listen to their conversation. Should she?

'I have been longing to see you. It takes a fire to do that – to allow me to see you,' a grinning Alice told Jerome.

'I am sorry. Has that man been bothering you?'

'Oh no, I pray to Massa God that he keeps away.'

'This fire will at least keep him busy.'

'I hope so. We should not be seen talking.'

'I know. I want you to hold me but it is not possible, eh?'

'Not now. This is maybe a good sign for us. The abolitionists are trying to make their presence known. It is only a matter of time, Alice. I want to hold you too but you know the consequences.'

'Don't worry, my love. It is only a matter of time. I better get going. Will you be at church on Sunday?'

'For sure. I could not miss that.'

'Good. Take care until then,' she smiled, telling him with her eyes that she really needed him.

The gathering of slaves in that particular spot was so

thick that both masters and foremen weren't able to see them.

Maude came up to Jerome; her sleepy eyes had a message of concern, 'Be careful.'

'We didn't speak for long,' Jerome said.

'Anita has been watching,' she said.

'What? How do you know that?'

'Because I have been watching her.'

'I don't think she suspects anything.'

'Maybe it is better she does.'

'What do you mean?'

'At least she will know that she is not alone.'

'Aunt Maude, that doesn't sound like you.'

'It doesn't?'

'How come?'

'It is probably getting too dangerous,' she said, concern in her voice.

'Since when did you realise that?'

'Tonight.'

'But tonight means things will change soon.'

'Probably, probably not.'

'She wants me and me alone, Aunty. She won't compromise and she won't give up now, not when things seem to be moving quicker than we thought.'

'I only want to tell you that you cannot be too careful.'

'I know, Aunty.'

Alfred's hands were signalling to his faithful flock that it was time to move back to his place. The fire was not as bright as it was before; they didn't have to waste any more time on it.

They came together quickly and followed their master's command of returning to quarters. Anita walked with her family, her mind picturing the little encounter her eyes had with Jerome and that beautiful young slave girl. She compared herself with her and wondered if Jerome had a choice, whom he would choose. Was anything going on? She hated the thought. Suppose something was in fact going on, how would she know?

'I didn't expect you to come,' Alfred told her.

'I couldn't stay in that house. I had to come.'

'As you can see my dear, the situation is going from bad to worse.'

'Slavery will be abolished, Dad. It is just a matter of time.'

Alfred looked at his daughter and wondered what was in her thoughts. 'How come you are so positive?'

'I have a gut feeling that a system like this cannot last for long.'

'Hmmm; how can a country like this... how can England afford to survive without its colonies, which thrive on slavery?'

'That is for the politicians to decide,' she said looking behind her, a number of torches giving light through the narrow track back to the house. John was nowhere in sight and she didn't bother to look for Jerome in the dark.

'There is nothing much we can do, my dear. We can only hope for the best.'

'I guess we'd better leave it at that, Dad. It is only time that will tell.'

'We cannot be too careful and I must emphasise that Lynda will have someone with her if she is going somewhere and you must too.'

'I will be all right, Dad.'

'I want to believe that.'

Lynda came closer to them, butting into the conversation. 'I don't even feel comfortable with you being around slaves,' she said.

'Mom, I feel safer with them than anything else. They won't hurt me.'

'You cannot assume that my dear. They are unpredictable, especially now when they are waging war in order to become free men.'

'That could still be a long way off and this might lead them to do things out of the ordinary,' Lynda said.

'Regardless of that, I don't feel threatened.'

'You should,' said Alfred. 'You see what happened here tonight.'

'But how can you be certain that it was done by slaves?'

'Well, let us assume that they are the ones who have a motive for doing it.'

'What motive?'

'They want to weaken us; they want us to give in to their demands but we will struggle to the end. We won't give up.'

Anita did not want to continue the conversation. All she could think about was that girl talking with Jerome. The more she thought about them the more she became jealous. Now she was being tempted to do something outrageous in order to get to the bottom of her suspicions.

What could she do? Suddenly she thought of another place where they could be together, in fact as often as they liked. That was probably what had been going on all along. Anita was convinced that she should pay a visit to their church next Sunday.

Chapter Twenty

A lingering fear hung over Big Yard for most of the week. Emancipation, abolition, freedom, justice were on the lips of many people – from slaves to masters. The fire at Larry's place brought home the prospect of an early breakthrough in the quest for freedom. Slaves were elated but their masters wore grim faces.

For the entire week John seemed to push the slaves harder than ever. He became more concerned about their freedom, and at the same time he never gave up on the idea that Anita probably did have someone in her life and it was his duty to find out. The person he had in mind was a long shot, yet he was determined to prove himself right.

On the other hand, Anita, too was determined to cover lost ground with Jerome. Her jealousy flared uncontrollably; it forced her to make every effort to see him. She couldn't wait until Sunday, she wanted to see him now, regardless of the consequences. She passed on her desire to Maude and although Maude was not too enthusiastic about the meeting tonight with Jerome, she did tell him about the planned rendezvous at Lookout.

Lookout was unusually chilly tonight. It was winter in the tropics, a cool seventy-two degrees. Anita dressed scantily in anticipation of some turbulent lovemaking. She could hardly wait.

Jerome came with the intention of having a little talk with Anita on the latest news circulating about a possible date for the abolition of slavery. Anita had other plans.

She grabbed him commandingly, clamping on to his lips as hard as ever. There was little Jerome could do but return the compliment. They lay in each other's arms, with Jerome's back against an almond tree providing support. They were so tired they couldn't even talk.

A pair of cold, angry and tearful eyes watched from behind a tree, all that had transpired for the past thirty-five minutes or so. The worst fears had now been confirmed. Anita's lover was a slave, and judging from what had happened here tonight, she was very much in love with him.

John was angrier than he could imagine. Yet he failed to understand how he didn't charge right up to that tree to break up that romantic scene. Right before his very eyes was the woman he loved in the arms of not just another man – a slave.

While John's restraint was unexplainable, he decided to leave as soon as they had finished. He wanted to see no more. In fact, he had seen too much.

The following night, Jerome found himself back at Hell House. The reason: none given. All he remembered was an angry and raging John barking at him, the first opportunity he got. He was not making any sense to Jerome and when he tried to find out what it was he was trying to say John claimed he was being rude.

The news about another night at Hell House reached Anita's ears quickly, through Maude. Anita, on hearing it, bolted into her father's study.

'Dad?' she said, as she entered the small room.

'Yes,' he said looking up from under the rim of his eyeglasses.

'Why are we being so unfair to Jerome?'

'Jerome? Who is Jerome?'

'The slave who takes us to Malvern sometimes.'

'The slave with whom you are in love.'

Anita stopped in her tracks. She felt as though a bolt of lightning had struck her. The words she wanted to use in reaction to her father's statement were not forthcoming. Anger was all over Alfred's face, and she needed no spectacles to see that he was angry all over.

'A-are y-you asking me, or are you telling me?' she managed to say.

'Does it make a difference? You tell me,' he snapped.

Once again, she found it somewhat difficult to respond. She hesitated.

'Well, are you going to answer me?' he said, rising from his seat like an interrogator.

No answer.

'I take it that you are admitting it,' he snarled, the anger boiling more and more, never seen to that level before by Anita.

Lynda walked into the room. She must have been listening. 'Anita, my dear, we need to know,' she said, coming up towards her from the rear.

'Why?' was all she could say.

'You mean to tell me that you are in love with a slave right on my own land and in this country where all the talk you can hear nowadays is about their freedom? They are ready to burn down the plantations and you, my only daughter are going to stand there and ask why?'

'Calm down Alfred, let us deal with this important matter in a more gentle way.'

'Calm down? Sorry but I cannot take this lying down.'

'I am in love with him and nothing will change that,' Anita blurted out.

Lynda's face twitched in shock; Alfred's eyes seemed to bulge out of his head.

'Over my dead body!' he yelled. 'You, in love with a slave? That can never be. Never! Not as long as I live.'

'Anita, my love,' said Lynda, holding her hand, 'are you

certain about this?'

'I am and nothing will change that, Mom.'

Alfred looked around at his daughter, rage gushing through every part of his being. Was he dreaming?

'That son of a bitch!' he yelled.

'Alfred, calm down.'

'That son of a bitch has been accompanying my daughter all around and I am here without even a clue as to what has been going on. He has to go!'

Anita whirled around at him. 'If he goes, I go too.'

'What? What are you talking about?' Alfred snapped.

'Let me repeat,' said Anita calmly, certain about what she had said. All she could think of now was Jerome and how much she really loved this slave. 'If you ever think of selling him forget it. Wherever he goes I will find him. The truth is I cannot live without him. I need him as much as he needs me – we cannot live without each other.'

Lynda was dumb. She sat there listening to her daughter, wondering if she had been hearing right.

'How long has this been going on Anita?' she asked.

'Around six months.'

'That's why you didn't want John?' Alfred asked, a little less anger in his voice.

'As I have told you before, John is not my type.'

'But a slave is?' he queried.

'I don't see him as a slave – just a nice young man who makes me feel like somebody.'

His anger flared again. This time, Alfred tried to be more forceful about his views on the subject. 'You can feel all you want Anita. You are under our care and I am telling you right now... right now that this relationship will have to end now whether you like it or not. I will not tolerate my daughter going around with a slave. Never! So you might as well forget him now because you won't see him any more.'

Alfred said no more. He grabbed his whip and stormed

out of the room. Anita and Lynda weren't even given a chance to respond. They stared after him; they saw in him today something they had never seen before.

He marched towards John's house, wondering what strategy to employ in order to get rid of the menace in his daughter's life.

John was sitting in his rocking chair puffing a cigar.

He greeted Alfred as if he was expecting him.

'How did it go?' he asked Alfred.

'She admitted it.'

'And?'

'Sh-she said she cannot live without him.'

'Huh? A slave?'

'She doesn't see him as a slave.'

'What? I wonder if something is wrong with her.'

Alfred's anger was rekindled. 'John, that is something I am trying very hard to understand. I cannot see why my daughter, of all people, should give her love to a slave... my property.'

'This is really a surprise.'

'You know a few weeks ago we were talking about her settling down and getting married. She told me one day she would give me a surprise regarding that. What better surprise?'

'Are you going to take it like that?'

'Over my dead body,' he emphasised.

'What then?'

'That is why I am here, John.'

'You need my help?'

'Yes.'

'I would be glad to help.'

'Good.'

'Where do we start?'

'With the slave. I was planning to sell him but I fear the consequences.'

'Of what?'

'Anita threatens that if I do, she will go too.'

'Go where?' asked John, a little troubled.

'Wherever he is going.'

'Are you serious?'

'I am.'

'I am thinking of isolating him.'

'How?'

'We must not send him to Hell House because that is when Anita apparently gets to see him.'

'That could be true. I have never thought of that at all and it could only make matters worse.'

'I will have him under guard at nights.'

'How are we going to do that?'

'He will sleep in the storehouse,' he said, indicating its presence behind him, just adjacent to John's quarters.

'There is a big padlock I can give you and that must go on at nights. He won't be able to come out. He will be the first one in the field and the last one to leave. And he will go on no more trips. For the time being, this is how I intend to keep Anita away from him.'

Alfred scratched his beard, nodding in approval. 'That sounds good to me. I guess if there is any further trouble on plantations in the area we might as well just sell him. But the way things are now, it is better to wait until things cool off a bit.'

'I think so too.'

★

Anita knew that sleep was far from her eyes. All night she had been restless. The thought of losing Jerome, of not seeing him again, was too much to bear. That was not possible, she told herself. When she thought of their ravenous lovemaking last night it made matters worse.

Someone must have seen them, she thought. John! It must have been him. He had been snooping around ever since she told him she was not interested in a relationship with him.

Now Anita feared what Alfred could do to Jerome. Poor Jerome, she thought. He didn't know what had happened tonight; if he did, then it could be the last of their relationship. There must be a way out, she told her confused self. She loved him more and more each time she saw him. She would probably even give her life for him; she would hate to see him in pain.

Anita was utterly confused. Questions of death, running away with him, giving up all she had for him, were now entering her mind. She felt sick in the stomach and in her mind. Her thoughts became a tangled web of confusion and uncertainty. She could not live without him. Thoughts of that nature had seeped into her mind the other night when she saw Jerome and Alice. Tonight they came with full force. What would she do now? Jerome must not feel any pain because of her. She had promised him that at the beginning of their relationship. Rather, it should be the other way around; she would take the pain on behalf of him.

*

Maude watched Anita stagger into the kitchen and she knew right away that something was wrong. For one, she woke up late, and another, the look on her face told Maude all was not well. Alfred and Lynda came earlier, and as soon as they had something to eat, they disappeared.

'Is everything okay Miss Anita?'

She looked at Maude without answering.

'I know something is wrong. You know you can talk to me.'

'I feel like I am going to die.'

'What? Do you feel sick?'

'The whole of my life is sick.'

'With what?'

'Love.'

'But that is good.'

'No, that is not good.'

'How?'

'Love is killing me.'

'How?' Maude repeated. She was puzzled.

'Dad knows about Jerome.'

'What? How?' Maude's eyes peered out at her. 'Are you joking?'

'I am not. John saw us last night and he told him.'

'Massa God have mercy! He is raving mad?'

'More than that. He wants us out of the relationship and he is threatening to sell Jerome.'

'Oh Massa God have mercy – my only son is going away, oh, the pain. Please God don't let it happen… please,' she moaned as she got down on her knees.

Anita was frightened at her sudden plunge into mourning. 'Don't worry, he won't do that,' she assured her. 'I told him if Jerome goes I go too.'

Maude looked up at her, relieved at her statement. She knew Alfred loved his daughter and wouldn't do anything to hurt her. She was convinced about that, and fortunately it made her feel much better.

'I cannot live without him Maude and Dad will have to understand that.'

'What will they do to him?'

'I don't know.'

★

Alice was looking forward to seeing Jerome on Sunday. Maybe he would have more news on the abolition movement – news that could give them much hope.

But suppose there was no good news? Could she continue to live with the prospect that any day the sex-starved Larry could bolt in on her and demand whatever he wanted?

The fire the other night could have been a blessing in disguise. Larry had been busy ever since trying to rebuild. It kept him busy and tired and Alice liked that. Her future was with Jerome and nothing could change that now. She was so glad to see him the other night. It was such a pity he had to go. She would have preferred to be with him all night, holding hands and talking about their future.

She continued to wash her master's dirt-stained clothes, wishing that one day it would be her husband's clothes that she would be washing. She smiled because that was what kept her going.

Chapter Twenty-One

Thunder rolled. The lightning opened up the sky to reveal thick, dark clouds that poured out rain from all over. The rain would last way into the night. There was no doubt about that. It had been falling all afternoon, non-stop.

Most of the slaves came from the field all soaked. By the time Jerome had changed into some new clothes and had something to eat, a grinning John came through the door. He looked around the room until his evil eyes rested on Jerome. He knew something was wrong. He beckoned to Jerome and he quickly rose to his feet and came over to him.

John didn't say anything. He grabbed his hand and led him out into the rain. Maude, frightened like a scared rabbit followed them to the door. It was dark outside now and it was only the flash of lightning that allowed her watery eyes to see when they entered the storehouse adjoining John's bunk. That would be Jerome's new home. Babwe came up beside her.

'They know,' he said quietly.

'Yes. It is better they put him over there than sell him.'

'Sell him?'

'Yes. Anita said they wanted to do that.'

'Please Massa God don't let that happen,' said a nervous Babwe looking into the ceiling towards heaven. 'I guess he will be sleeping there from now on.'

'I would imagine so. Let us hope we hear some good news soon.'

'That may be our only chance.'

In the morning John brought Jerome over on his way to the field. He had to gulp down his breakfast of porridge and bread in order to leave with them almost right away.

A sensitive Jerome didn't have to ask why his new sleeping quarters would be in the storehouse beside John. He had heard him put on the padlock and it was then he knew that they meant business. What did Anita have to do with all of what was happening?

It didn't take long for him to find out. Over dinner, Maude told it all.

Jerome was trembling. He was afraid but relieved that Alfred hadn't taken more drastic action. He agreed that it was due in part to Anita. Alfred didn't want to hurt her.

Jerome pitied himself as well as Anita. He felt as though he truly loved her now, and that the love Anita had for him was undying. Would he ever see her again? That seemed unlikely, at least for now.

He realised her pain now. The fact that she had to face up to her father with the startling truth about their love was enough to cause her stress and grief. Knowing the sort of strong-willed person Anita was, Jerome sensed that she probably wasn't afraid of confessing her love for a slave. She must bear the consequences now, if any, that would follow the revelation. Most likely, the price she would pay would be never to see him again.

As for Jerome, he knew that further action could be taken against him. He thought of Alice and he was confused no more. There was the likelihood that he wouldn't even be allowed to go to church. Or, he could go to confess his sins – Alfred would see that he did that – and to start anew. Slaves were sometimes afforded that opportunity. The sacrifice that Anita made in confessing their love did have an impact over Jerome. He came to respect her even more. She loved him. That was clear to him.

If there was a future now with Alice, he could not see it at the present moment. It must be a few years down the line. He would have to tell her that if he was allowed to go to church on Sunday. Anita had done a lot, maybe too much, and despite him being a slave, Jerome wanted to make it up to her. That was what he thought about all night in the lonely confines of the storehouse. He fell asleep on those thoughts.

Maude had told Anita about what had been done to Jerome. She was relieved it was not something worse than that. A few minutes before she saw Maude, Alfred, who was still angry with her, told Anita that he wouldn't be selling Jerome but while he was still his property she would not see him again. If she did, it would be the last of him. He also threatened to send her back to England with Lynda if she refused to obey.

Anita was convinced that all of that was useless. She had to see Jerome at all costs. She had to face the fact that she could not live without him. She would be better off dead.

Another night in her lonely bed with the man she loved locked away in darkness was too much for Anita. All kinds of possibilities and temptations ran through her mind.

She could feel her stomach churning for lack of food; her appetite was lost to a world of confusion. So confused she was that thoughts of dying, rather than living without him, even entered her mind.

She marched around her room in the darkness glancing down into the pitch blackness of the night. The storehouse was not visible from that view, yet she visualised Jerome coiled up on either grass or the bare ground. Her blood warmed for his; her lips parted in awe when she remembered the more passionate moments.

How could she live without such a man, slave or free? Life never meant anything real until the night they first kissed. All that had been taken away now by her very own parents and John, whom she thought at one time was her only friend in the world.

She flung herself down on the bed, tears streaming across her face. She cried silently, then it became a little louder, then louder and louder, until she could cry no more. She cried herself to sleep.

Maude was as worried as Babwe. She looked across at him, her dinner untouched.

'What do you think will happen to him?' he asked. Babwe couldn't be more serious, something which was out of character for him.

'I believe they will sell him,' she said dryly.

'Sell him? Y'know I never even thought about that.'

'That is what worries me.'

'Now that you mention it, I am a little concerned too but...'

Maude looked up at him. 'But what?'

'If Anita really loves him do you think Massa Campbell would just get rid of him like that?' he said, scratching his beard.

'Remember he is a slave.'

'I know, but Massa Campbell only cares about his daughter, nothing else. He is not going to hurt her.'

'I wish that was so.'

'I have a feeling it is,' he said with a little more confidence.

'Babwe, you only want me to feel better.'

'Well let us wait and see what happens before jumping to any conclusions.'

'But he is hurting.'

'I know.'

'There isn't much more we can do than encourage him that everything will work out fine.'

'Knowing him, right now he is more worried about Anita than himself.'

'He should be more concerned about himself.'

'I wish he was.'

'He genuinely loves her and doesn't want to see her get hurt.'

'Then there's Alice – the girl I was telling you about.'

'She is crazy over him too?'

'Yes. Her future with him now seems to be in limbo.'

'He has to get himself out of this one first.'

'If John allows him to.'

'He is the one playing with fire because Miss Anita turned him down. If it wasn't for him, everything would have been going as planned.'

'I know. That fat pig.'

Maude barely smiled. 'I am wondering if I should speak to Massa.'

Babwe was dumbstruck. 'Woman! You hit the nail on the head. That is an idea. It may not work but at least you could say you did try.'

'Exactly what I am thinking,' she said with a clenched fist.

'You work so hard for him and I know he has a little respect for you, Maude. You are his longest serving employee. Doesn't that mean something?'

'I sure hope it does.'

★

Maude went out of her way to prepare a good breakfast for Alfred. He came through the kitchen door looking rather tired.

'Are you ready for me Maude?' he asked.

'Sure. Are you waiting on Miss Lynda?'

'No, she is still sleeping. She will be down later.'

Maude pushed the plate before him; all decorated with fried plantains, his favourite, a fried egg, a strip of home-made bacon, fried dumplings, a slice of bread, and a steaming cup of black coffee.

'This surely looks good. I have not eaten a good meal in days.'

'Worried about Miss Anita?' she said, without even wondering if she was invading private affairs. But knowing the openness and the close relationship she had with her master, she took the chance.

Alfred's expression remained unchanged. 'Oh boy, you can say that again.'

'I am worried too, about my son.'

'S-son... well I am sorry about that.'

'I worry, Massa, because I don't know what will happen to my son.'

'Nothing will happen Maude. I am not certain what I will do about him. I have to admit I was very angry when I took the decision to lock him up.'

Maude was relieved. 'Then you could release him again?'

'I would want to think so.'

'Thank you sir, and now sit comfortably and have a hearty breakfast.'

'Can you do me a favour Maude?'

'Anything to keep my son.'

Alfred's face lit up as he chewed on the fried dumpling. 'Will you tell him to leave my daughter alone? You know how it is on this island. There is no future for the two of them. She is white and free and he is a slave.'

'I will talk to him, sir. I hope he comes to his senses.'

'Good, he can return to his bunk.'

★

Jerome had feared another night in the storehouse. Now he was told by Maude that he would not be going there tonight.

'What happened?' a relieved Jerome asked Maude.

'I begged for you.'

Jerome got up from his seat and came round the table to Maude and hugged her tightly. 'You are a real mother to me.'

'A real mother will do anything for her son.'

'You have proved that many times. How can I ever make up for this latest one?'

'I made Massa Alfred a promise.'

'About me?'

'Yes.'

'What, Aunt Maude?'

'That you will stop seeing Miss Anita.'

The words fell on Jerome's ear like a thunderball.

'Can you?'

Jerome looked away. Sadness and pain were in his squinting eyes. 'Aunt Maude, I don't want to hurt her.'

'She loves you, eh?'

'To death.'

'And you love her?'

'I love her more than anything.'

'What about Alice?'

Again, Jerome turned away his head. He looked back at Maude. 'I love her too.'

'Anita is forbidden love, Jerome. It is a love not for this age. Look at the whole situation, my son. It won't work. Sorry I did not see it like that before. You are a slave and she is a free woman who can get anyone she wants. My son, it is a love for tomorrow. Alice is waiting for you.'

Babwe came over to join them. 'Take our advice son and don't see her again.'

'You too, Babwe?' Jerome mumbled. 'I thought I had your support.'

'You had it once my son but under the circumstances we

don't want to lose you.'

'Lose me? How?'

'He would probably have sold you.'

'What?'

'Yes. That is why we are afraid,' said Maude.

'Do you all know what love is?' Jerome said bluntly.

Maude looked at Babwe.

'I have that feeling. I know what it is – true love, regardless of who we are.'

'Are you crazy?' Maude asked, her voice echoing in the small surroundings. 'Jerome, look at me.' He did. 'You are playing with fire. Massa Campbell said you must not see her anymore and if you want to stay around here you better do as he says. It would be better with Alice.'

'Maybe I can't even see Alice any more. We could be free soon. Does that mean when I am a free man I won't be able to see Alice too?'

'That is still a little way off,' Babwe said. 'Don't bet your life on it, at least not for now.'

'I probably won't but the two of you must understand I have a life to live; no disrespect – I am grateful for your advice but all I can say now is that I don't see a life without Anita or Alice.'

Maude and Babwe stared at Jerome and they knew he meant every word he had said. They wished he was telling a lie.

Chapter Twenty-Two

The more Anita thought about it the more she was convinced that it was the only way out for her and Jerome. What they had here was not working, hence any other plan should.

The next time she saw Jerome she must convince him that they should run away to another part of the island; probably Spanish Town. She could pose as a rich white woman and Jerome, her slave. Anita knew where her father kept his money. That would not be a problem. The only problem was to convince Jerome they should take the chance. Slavery could soon be abolished and things could get brighter for them. She must find a way to see him now.

Somehow, Maude did not feel like going to church on such a bright Sunday morning. Normally she would have, but when Jerome asked her to carry the heavy burden of telling Alice everything, she had little choice. She understood Jerome's position.

She must help her son in whatever way she could, and when she thought about that she concluded that probably the best thing for him now was to give the two women in his life a break. That was a good enough reason for her to talk to Alice for him.

Alice was standing in the church's doorway when Maude walked up.

'He isn't coming, is he? Something is wrong – I can sense it.'

'You are right, my dear,' she said solemnly.

'What is it?' Alice asked calmly.

'I-I d-don't know how to tell you this...'

'Go ahead,' she said, with even more calm in her soft voice.

'He is in big trouble.'

'For what?'

Maude hesitated somewhat. She could feel the pain that was about to crawl throughout her nervous system. 'Massa Alfred's daughter...'

'What? What about her?'

Maude waited until what she had said registered fully. 'They said Jerome an' she have something going.'

'J-Jerome! Jerome! Th-that can't be... Jerome? My Jerome? They must be mistaken. Am I hearing right?'

'You are.'

'Tell me they are wrong, Maude.'

'I am afraid it's true.'

'Y-you really mean it?' Tears came, and more, and more until she could no longer look at Maude. She must see Jerome right away. Her stomach burned with jealousy – something she had never realised until now. All kinds of thoughts raced through her mind in that instant. To live with the thought that her beloved Jerome was in the arms of another woman would be too much for her. Alice felt like she could kill, or be killed defending the love of her life – a very deep love she had only been discovering since Maude's revelation to her. Today was a day Alice felt like she would break all the rules in order to preserve her only true love. Would she be successful? Didn't Jerome promise her sincerely he wouldn't hurt her? Yet Alice was hurt more than ever. So hurt that she acted as though she was going insane. She stepped past Maude, sobbing uncontrollably. She wished tomorrow was Sunday.

★

Lynda had been depressed all week and Sunday was no exception. For Alfred, it was no better. On a number of occasions he started out with the intention of grabbing Jerome and taking him into Malvern for sale. Over the past two days, his anger intensified and he told himself the next time he saw Jerome he would be capable of doing anything.

Alfred hardly saw his daughter all week. She had been avoiding him; likewise, he did the same. Anita was hurting and he knew it. But it was better she grieved that way rather than planned her future around a slave.

It was Sunday again and Jerome wanted to go to church to clear his mind. However, Alice's lovely face haunted him. He had promised not to hurt her and now she must have heard. If his relationship with Anita had to be stopped then Alice would always be there. He had been dreaming of her all week; and to make matters worse, he hadn't seen her last Sunday at church.

Jerome had been trying to avoid his master too. John had been eyeing him like a hawk, watching his every move, and he knew today would probably be no exception.

'Going to church son?' Maude asked him. 'I think you should try to see Alice. She is really broken up y'know.'

Jerome looked up at her from the table at which he was sitting. 'I want to, Aunt Maude.'

'Then do it son. She loves you to death. She is going to go crazy!'

'It is that bad, eh?' Jerome's eyes never left hers.

'Uh-uh to be honest, son. She is capable of doing any-thing now. I don't know if she has recovered since last Sunday but when I saw her she was one crazy woman. She probably didn't know how much you mean to her.'

'Aunt Maude,' Jerome said, images flashing through his mind, 'are you leaving right... right now?' he said trium-phantly.

'Yes. Why?' What are going to do? Are you coming to

church?'

'No. But I have to see her. Tell her to meet me at Lookout as soon as possible. Tell her don't bother to go to church. I want to see her – I have to see her. I don't think I want to see Anita again.'

'You are certain about this my son?' Maude, wide-eyed, had a sense of relief. Finally, he was coming to his senses.

'I couldn't be more certain. All week, she has been in my dreams. It wasn't Anita. It was Alice and I want to make up to her. She will come, Aunty. I know that. She loves me. I was a fool not to have seen that.'

'What will you tell Anita?'

'I probably won't see her again, and if I do, I don't know what will happen. That will take care of itself.'

'I have to go. I have to tell her all you have said.'

Jerome rose from the table and kissed Maude. 'Thanks for helping me to come to my senses.'

'You did it all by yourself, with a little waking up of course.'

'Pray for me, Aunty.'

'I will son. Massa God be with you.'

Jerome walked to the door as soon as Maude had left. No one was in the big yard. It was all so quiet and calm. The breeze from the sea and Lookout was cool. The trees waved under pressure from it as if they were saying good-bye.

Jerome slipped out of the doorway and headed for Lookout, too anxious to see Alice. He hoped to God that Anita, Alfred, or John didn't see him. Not that it mattered greatly but he would have preferred not to see any of them. He had a gut feeling Alfred wanted to sell him and there was little Anita could do. Jerome hated that thought. He was convinced that it was over with Anita and to be separated from Alice again would be too much for him to handle – and probably for Alice too.

Alice hadn't changed much since Maude saw her last Sunday. She remained far from calm and all that was on her mind was Jerome. Maude sat her down on a bench at the back of the church and patiently told her all that Jerome had said. Her countenance started to transform when she got a hint at where the conversation was heading. Before Maude could even finish her presentation, Alice was getting up to go.

Maude was relieved; tears of joy crawled down her cheeks. About a dozen yards away, another face was washing in joyful tears. The faster Alice ran, the more the tears came. In less than ten minutes, she was in Jerome's arms at Lookout. She ran through Alfred's yard, without even looking to see if anyone was around. She never even noticed her master Larry standing on the steps of the house with Alfred and John. Near the big star apple tree, Hell House, Anita had been sitting on a bench there in one of her many manoeuvres to avoid her father. All eyes turned to see Alice running like a horse with blinkers.

Jerome saw her coming. The look in her eyes was one of hunger but not for food. Jerome was hungry, too, and he could wait no longer for the true love he had been blind to all along. Without even thinking of the consequences, Jerome hurled himself from the rock he had been sitting on and jumped three feet to solid ground. He lost his balance and when he regained it, he ran straight into the arms of Alice.

They couldn't say much because the thirst for each other's mouths was unbearable. And so the kisses started and continued unabated. When their mouths were tired, they clung to each other like magnets. As soon as they felt like releasing their grip, they both knelt on the ground, holding each other tightly, never letting go.

Something moved in the background and it caught Jerome's eyes. Alice withdrew slightly and looked after him.

Standing in the pathway were some figures they hadn't expected. The authoritative figures of their two masters, John and Anita, stared at them. Anita's mouth was half-opened and the look on their master's faces was far from friendly. Memories of her master's hand on her reminded Alice she was in big trouble. John had a machete in his hand apparently ready for a fight. They moved closer.

'My G-God, they are going to k-kill us,' whispered Alice, who had been clinging to Jerome.

'Th-they are going to t-t-take away our l-love sweet-heart. They can't! They can't Jerome. Tell them! tell them!' she trembled.

Jerome was nervous and he was frightened. He stepped backwards; they all moved closer.

'Over my dead body!' snarled Alfred. They all nodded in approval, except Anita, who started to back away from her father.

'Run Jerome! Run and leave her! It's you they are after, not her. Run for your life,' Anita yelled.

Alfred looked at his daughter. 'Get back to the house!' he snapped. Anita stood her ground.

'Don't leave me, d-don't…' mumbled Alice, huge sobs blurting out.

Jerome was crying too.

'Wherever you go I will go, Jerome. I love you and if you are going to die I am prepared to die for you.'

She looked at him and Jerome knew she meant it. He kissed her, regardless of the intruders around. In one flash, he grabbed Alice and lifted her on to the highest rock on which they could stand. They could see the roaring waves below and the mountains stretching down and down until they seemed to run into the sea.

Alice and Jerome had nowhere else to run. They both looked down at the shoreline glistening at them miles below. They looked at each other and knew they were thinking alike. It was now or never. She was willing to die for him and Jerome realised then that the woman whose love had meant so much to him in these last few moments, he was willing to die for too.

'Don't jump Jerome, I love you!' Anita screamed.

'Shut up, and go now!' an angry Alfred snorted.

John tried to steer her towards the house but she shoved him away. John gave up on that task. The two masters were only a few feet away from their slaves and it was only then they saw it coming.

The young slaves hugged each other tightly and kissed long and hard. They all stared in anger. John stepped forward with the machete. It was either that he wanted to grab them or to chop at them. Jerome and Alice had already made up their minds.

'I love you to death, Jerome and we will meet again in true love.'

'I love you too, Alice and forgive me for taking so long to see that,' he smiled, knowing she had forgiven him.

She returned the smile and just as Anita screamed 'No!' they kissed again and leapt right over the cliff.

Panicking, the onlookers jumped up on to the rock they had been standing on and looked over the cliff to see any sign of life. Trees and rocks blocked their view and from what they could see, the lovers couldn't have survived that fall.

They all looked at each other in silence. Anita stomped her feet, dashed herself on the ground and cried loudly. Alfred kept shaking his head. There began the legend of the lovers who leapt to their deaths, rather than living without each other.